FLAME LILY

MARY FAULKNER

THORNDIKE
CHIVERS

This Large Print edition is published by Thorndike Press, Waterville, Maine, USA and by BBC Audiobooks Ltd, Bath, England.
Thorndike Press is an imprint of Thomson Gale, a part of The Thomson Corporation.
Thorndike is a trademark and used herein under license.

The text of this Large Print edition is unabridged.
Other aspects of the book may vary from the original edition.
Set in 16 pt. Plantin.

LIBRARY OF CONGRESS CATALOGING-IN-PUBLICATION DATA

Faulkner, Mary.
   Flame Lily / by Mary Faulkner. — Large print ed.
     p. cm. — (Thorndike Press large print candlelight)
   ISBN-13: 978-0-7862-9467-1 (hardcover : alk. paper)
   ISBN-10: 0-7862-9467-1 (hardcover : alk. paper)
   1. Stepsisters — Fiction. 2. Large type books. I. Title.
PS3606.A867F57 2007
813'.6—dc22   2007002868

BRITISH LIBRARY CATALOGUING-IN-PUBLICATION DATA AVAILABLE

Published in 2007 in the U.S. by arrangement with Robert Hale Limited.
Published in 2007 in the U.K. by arrangement with Robert Hale Limited.

U.K. Hardcover: 978 1 405 64036 7 (Chivers Large Print)
U.K. Softcover: 978 1 405 64037 4 (Camden Large Print)

Printed in the United States of America on permanent paper
10 9 8 7 6 5 4 3 2 1

FLAME LILY

ONE

The passenger in the seat beside Tina on the jet heading south from Heathrow had kept himself aloof from the beginning. A clean-cut, tanned and firm-jawed type with something weighing on his mind, she had judged, after a quick appraisal under lowered lashes when he first took his place, with not so much as a glance in acknowledgement of her polite smile. Feeling rebuffed, she returned to her own private preoccupations which concerned this trip of hers back to the country of her birth. A reluctant trip. A wedding trip. And quite suddenly she didn't want to think about it.

Her fellow-passenger had ducked behind the evening paper, showing a glimpse now and then of his ruggedly handsome profile, but no sign of the friendliness customary between people on long-distance flights. After a while she wondered sarcastically whether the first-class had been full, forcing him to rough it back here doing his best to ignore those he might term 'the peasants'. Her long-lashed glance swept over him once more. Prosperity showed in his clothes, his excellent shoes, his grooming. The air of aloofness was something else. It was downright intriguing. And vaguely annoying.

Dinner-trolleys came down the aisles, serving out trays of food and a small bottle of wine on each; white for her, red for the man at her elbow, although he had previously ordered whisky and was swallowing it in his absent, preoccupied way which caused Tina an inward giggle, wondering whether he might be composing poetry, or perhaps plotting some nefarious business deals behind that withdrawn air of his. Well, good luck to him! She sipped her wine, peering through the tiny window at stars pricking through a black velvet sky, and tried to mind her own business.

Tina Andersons's incurable curiosity about life and people in general had attracted her to a journalistic career, which led to a position on the editorial staff of a woman's magazine and to trying her talents at short-story writing; all of it in London, which she loved. Life seemed to have become near-perfect at last after a troublesome childhood in the distant country once known as Rhodesia — now Zimbabwe — to which her parents had years ago emigrated from England, before the violence out there began. Soon afterwards her mother died, and then her father married a widow, and thus Tina was presented with a step-sister almost her own age, named Jade.

At the outbreak of the Rhodesian war, Jade and herself, as children, were packed off to relatives in England where both had grown up. Jade had since built for herself a successful modelling career in America, having first made her mark in London with all the style and panache of her winning personality. Furthermore, Jade was soon to be married. Her mother had insisted on having the wedding in Zimbabwe, with Tina supporting her step-sister as chief bridesmaid. One did not argue with Jade's mother, Rhoda, which was why Tina was flying to Africa when she would rather not. She owed it to Jade anyway, for old times' sake.

For Tina there was a touch of sadness in returning to a home she barely remembered, especially since her father had been killed in the Rhodesian war and her stepmother, a woman of Dutch descent, had married a new husband from Holland named Gerrit van Tonder, whom Tina had not yet met. Neither she nor Jade had been back since their departure from home as children, and now both were on recall for the wedding of Jade to a man about whom her mother had been mysteriously obscure. It was to be a surprise, she had informed Tina by letter, causing a suspicion that the intrusive Rhoda had pulled off some kind of coup. 'Your future brother-in-law is someone you know very well,' was the most Rhoda would divulge, adding, 'Come and see for yourself.' And Jade, from America, had been just as secretive.

Tina shrugged, leaning back in her seat on the aircraft. So here she was, off to Harare, that was once Salisbury, bearing a bridesmaid's dress from Harrods in her luggage and not caring very much at all who it was that Jade had decided to marry. Her fare had been paid and she was to be afforded a brief holiday in Zimbabwe before returning to London. 'We must try to find you a husband while you're out here,' Rhoda had written, to which Tina had not replied, not even to humour her stepmother.

Humouring Rhoda was a habit carried forward from the time when Tina and her father had shared their home with the ex-widow and her daughter, without Rhoda actually taking the place of her own mother in Tina's affections, nor in her father's either, Tina liked to imagine. It had, however, been a perfectly workable and pleasant arrangement for most of the time. The two girls had got on fairly well, due mainly to Tina's equable nature as against Jade's often stormy temperament. Together they weathered their school-days in England, drawing closer in times of trouble or homesickness. Rhoda came over to visit them a few times but loathed the English climate and cut short her stays.

The girls eventually launched into lives of their own, following different careers, the bond between them becoming increasingly tenuous, especially after Jade went to blaze a trail for herself in the fashion world of New York. Beautiful, self-assured Jade seemed born for success and happiness in a life smoothed of all obstacles. Tina, in her thoughtful moments, wondered if there really was such a thing as a perpetually smooth life? Or whether at some stage there came a day of reckoning in even the easiest style of existence.

She glanced again at the man in the neighbouring seat, now wearing headphones and lounging back, eyes shut, with the air of enjoying sublime music. Totally unsociable towards her, as he would *not* be if it were Jade sitting beside him! No man ever glanced past Jade, or gave her a cool, polite smile, as this one did so suddenly now that Tina was caught off guard. They gazed frankly at each other for a few moments during which she noticed that his eyes were a steely shade of grey, under heavily defined brows as black almost as his thick hair, grey-ing slightly at the temples. His body, so sinuously at ease in his seat, hinted at muscles that would be ready in a flash for quick, reflex action when required.

Before she could assemble a smile to match his for coolness, he closed his eyes again and went back to Rachmaninov, or whatever.

So much for that! Tina tilted her seat back for the night, shut her own eyes and pre-pared for rest, hindered by kinetic scenes produced by her over-active mind that kept playing across her closed lids; scenes sharp and clear of only yesterday, and others blurred and misty of countryside under a hot African sun, remembered from years ago. A lion walking towards her out of long grass. Her father raising his hunting-gun. She had been very sorry to see the lion drop. It had seemed to her childish mind almost like a friendly, outsized dog.

Sleep overcame her suddenly. Someone gently unfolded an airways blanket over her.

She snuggled sideways, found a comfortable head-rest and fell into deep exhausted sleep.

Sunlight shafting through the window was warming her lap when she awoke to sounds of movement around her; the clink of crockery, cheerful stewardess voices down and up the aisles. There was a feeling of roughness under her right cheek. It came as a surprise to discover her head resting on a shoulder — someone else's shoulder and a broad one at that. Her eyes flew open and met the supporting arm that was taking her weight.

'Good morning.' The husky voice came from just above her head and she felt the warmth of lips against her hair. She jerked herself upright as the truth dawned.

'Had a restful night?' enquired the man beside her, rubbing his arm with a wicked grin.

Tina felt herself turning bright red. She stammered an apology and mentioned that his arm must be quite numb.

The smile in his eyes mocked her. 'My arm has never been put to better service.'

'You should have awakened me.'

'Would never have dreamt of being that cruel.'

Grabbing her handbag she stood up, annoyed at feeling flustered and at a disadvantage out of all proportion with the occasion.

'Excuse me,' she said, tripping past the man before he had time to rise and make way. Like some gauche schoolgirl, she fumed at herself, bewildered by the confusion she felt.

There was a long queue outside the washroom, but at last it was her turn to dash water over her face, apply cleanser, a touch of fresh make-up and a quick spray of cologne. Now she felt better able to cope with the embarrassment of having slept the night on a stranger's shoulder — the shoulder of that arrogant, grey-eyed man of all people!

She caught her breath in shock as a new thought struck her. Was it he who had so carefully tucked the blanket over her?

Breakfast-trolleys were advancing down the aisles as she made her way. She found her seat-neighbour cheerfully munching toast from his tray, which he at once picked up to stand aside out of her way, and she acknowledged him with a self-contained smile as she settled in her seat. No sooner was her own tray brought, however, than the aircraft began lurching violently through a patch of turbulence. Coffee slopped over and the cup itself seemed about to rise in the air, but her neighbour's hand shot out to steady it. She had time to notice his long, lean fingers before they deftly moved now to her seat-belt fastening, just in time to counter a particularly sharp downward lurch. 'Belt up,' he said, indicating the red light.

She grabbed hold of his hand during the falling sensation and hung on to it in the shake-up that followed. He smiled reassuringly down at her, his eyes creased attractively at the corners. She noticed how much younger he really was than the silvered temples suggested. And not in the least stand-offish now. His grey eyes had developed warm depths as they gazed at each other.

'Will it remain as bumpy as this all the way?' she shakily asked.

'Oh, no. It'll soon pass,' he comforted.

'I suppose you've flown this route before?'

'Yes.'

'Often?' She was talking at random to keep her mind off the bucking bronco they were trapped in.

'No. Not often,' he said.

'Sorry to be so inquisitive. And — and for using your shoulder as a pillow last night.'

'My shoulder quite enjoyed it.'

Tina discovered she was still clutching his hand and hastily let go. He calmly lifted his coffee-cup with the freed hand and drained it. 'End of turbulence,' he remarked, casually leaning across so that his cheek lightly touched hers while he took a long look through the window. 'Salisbury down there,' he pointed. 'No — correction. Harare down there. It's the new name they've given it.'

Tina followed his gaze but the plane veered now to a view of distant hills.

'The Vumba Mountains,' her companion said. He turned to her abruptly and asked, 'Are you staying long?'

'No. I'm only here for a wedding.'

She was surprised at the sudden sharpening of his eyes on her, a raising of the eyebrows. There seemed almost to be a look of dawning recognition on his face although that seemed impossible.

'So? Well now, that's a coincidence,' he said.

'Why?' Tina frowned, meeting his eyes.

'Because so am I. Here for a wedding.'

16

Two

A group of spectators had assembled on the terrace at Harare airport to watch the incoming flight. Among them Tina imagined she recognized Rhoda, a slightly tubby, middle-aged figure dressed in flowered polyester, waving importantly as the jet taxied up.

'I believe that might be my stepmother,' she remarked to the man at her side, whose name had not yet been mentioned although they had been chatting pleasantly for some minutes. Questions mostly. His questions, her replies.

'Oh really?' he drawled, seeming resentful of the interruption. 'A pity we didn't get sociable sooner. I'd like to hear much more about you.'

Whereas, she thought, he had told her nothing about himself. She became suddenly quiet, raising her eyes to his: 'I don't even know your name.'

'Oh — sorry. It's Scott. Scott Kyle. And this, I fear, is the end of our journey. Here, let me help with your case and things.'

Tina watched him get busy and thought what a remarkable change had come over the man. This new side of him was really very likeable.

He remained with her helpfully throughout disembarkation and Customs procedures, his hand placed lightly over her waist to guide her along, until they were done with formalities and out of the building.

And there was Rhoda at the entrance to the car-park, flapping her elbows like some plump bird about to attempt flight and calling out 'Here! Here I am!' As if one could possibly miss her. She made a sudden rush towards them.

Tina stood expecting to receive her stepmother's embrace, but stumbled aside as Rhoda pushed past and flung her arms around Scott. 'Dear, dear boy! How perfectly lovely to see you!' And then, releasing him suddenly she turned to Tina. 'You might have told me you were travelling together.'

'It's you who might have told us,' Scott laughed off her brusqueness, with a wink at Tina. 'You made the plans.'

'But you were due to arrive *tomorrow,*

18

Scott. Tina was to come ahead, and Jade will be here — in a couple of days I believe.'

'Oh,' said Scott. 'Well, you might introduce the pair of us now, Rhoda.'

Rhoda frowned, then recovered herself and said, 'Oh, well, Scott, this is my stepdaughter Tina Anderson. And Tina, this is Scott Kyle, as you ought to know. Surely you remember him?'

Tina cast a startled glance at Scott. 'Should I?'

'Good heavens,' said Rhoda impatiently, 'you were youngsters growing up here just a few years ago. Although, of course, Scott was rather senior to you two girls.'

'Twenty years ago,' said Scott drily. 'We've all changed since then.'

'As for myself, I feel as young as ever,' Rhoda informed them coyly. 'But come along, let's get you home. It must have been a tiring flight.'

Rhoda led them to one of the parked cars where she turned suddenly and faced them with an oddly triumphantly smile.

'Well, Tina, this is the surprise I've had in store for you. Scott is the man Jade is to marry.'

Tina drew a sharp breath and stopped dead. Scott, a pace or two ahead, turned and looked at her.

Rhoda let out a high note of laughter. 'She certainly is surprised, isn't she, Scott? And now Tina, give your future brother-in-law a nice warm welcoming kiss, child.'

Tina made no move until Rhoda tugged her forward by the hand and pushed her at Scott. His arms came out to encircle her.

Their lips brushed lightly at first, and then all at once it was as if they were alone, poised on the brink of something cataclysmic and irrevocable. Scott's mouth pressed down hard on hers and she found herself returning his kiss with equal fervour and rising passion, closing her eyes and going limp.

'Well, now, I'd say that was enough.' Rhoda's voice held a tone of surprise and sharpness. Opening the car's front door she announced to the slowly separating couple: 'I'll drive. Scott will sit in front with me and Tina in the back seat. Come along.' They were hustled off.

Rhoda's driving was erratic, and she kept up a stream of talk, glancing only occasionally at the road ahead. Tina remembered how the slightest excitement in her stepmother's life made a compulsive talker of her and brought out her Dutch-colonial tendency to use Afrikaans sentences mingled with English, running words together in the Afrikaaner manner.

The forthcoming wedding had evidently stirred Rhoda to fever pitch. '*Ag* shame!' she enthused, 'isn't it too wonderful for my Jade and Scott to be getting together! They were meant for each other, weren't they, Tina?'

'By the way,' Scott interrupted. 'Why is Jade delayed?'

The question seemed to throw Rhoda off balance for a moment. The car swerved sharply towards the roadside ditch before she recovered, with a frivolous little laugh. 'Man! I never realised how hard they make models work. First-class models, that is. *Successful* models, like my daughter, don't seem to have time to breathe. Jade was so *upset* when she phoned from New York yesterday to say she wouldn't be able to catch her flight.'

'Why?' the word shot from Jade's fiancé. 'Why exactly?'

'Now, Scott, just you stop worrying. Everything's fine. It's just that some urgent assignment turned up which she had to fulfil. She'll be on another flight just as soon as possible.'

The car veered again as Rhoda glanced back at Tina in the rear. 'This man is bursting with impatience to see his love. We'll have to be gentle with him, Tina.'

Scott gave a sudden yell. 'Hey! Look out! Phew, we almost wrote off that donkey-cart.' He looked back through the window to confirm that the rickety old cart and driver were intact.

'Shame,' said Rhoda lugubriously, patting his shoulder. 'I can see you're all nerves and disappointment, my boy. Not to mention jet lag. You must have a nice rest. Jade is relying on me to take care of you for her. We're nearly there now.'

It was obvious from Scott's disagreeable grunt that he was in no mood to be pacified with mommy-talk. The signals were that he was a disappointed and irritable lover. Jade had better delay no longer, Tina thought.

The road now wound through a settlement of houses set in lawns and gardens. Rhoda turned the car into an open gateway, followed a gravelled path round a group of eucalyptus trees and stopped alongside the front verandah steps.

An African wearing the white drill uniform of a houseboy came down the steps and busied himself with the luggage. Tina was immediately struck by some old memory as she watched his grizzled head bobbing in and out of the open boot of the car.

'Matches!' she cried in sudden recognition and pleasure. 'Is it really you?'

The elderly man straightened up to flash her a wide grin. 'Yes, missy. Me still here for little time longer.'

'He keeps talking about retirement but we won't let him go,' Rhoda thrust herself into the reunion between Tina and the servant who had been with her parents from the beginning, and had been taken over by Rhoda and her new husband.

Tina grasped the old servant's hand. 'I'm so happy to see you again, Matches. How are your wife and children?'

'Two wives, eight children. Picannins all grown up now. Welcome home, missy.' Matches respectfully withdrew his hand at sight of Rhoda's critical look.

Tina was nudged by her stepmother, who had her arm linked through Scott's, and Scott was given first turn at being shown his room while Tina waited in the sitting-room, gazing about quietly. It was the same room she had known in childhood, but with no memories of her own mother, because this was the new house her father had bought before his marriage to Rhoda.

Rhoda came bustling in, talking all the while. 'So here you are back home again. And what an occasion this is going to be for us all!' She had put on weight, and her dark hair, permed and meticulously set, had glints of grey showing, though they had been tinted blonde. She was still a good-looking woman, determined to be kindly and protective towards her step-daughter. Together they went towards Tina's allotted room.

Tina began a question and faltered: 'How is . . . How is, er —' Neither she nor Jade had been able to call Rhoda's husband 'Father', nor even 'Dad' and there was always this hesitation before ending up with 'Pops', an alternative suggested by Mr van Tonder himself in one of his earlier letters to the girls in England.

'Oh, Gerrit is very well, as usual. A fit man always, I'm glad to say. He'll be home this evening from a trip to Bulawayo. It's a responsible position for him, being manager of one of our largest department stores, but he takes it all in his stride. Of course nowadays they are training African managers for such jobs so it might not be long before —' Rhoda broke off and shrugged, and lit a cigarette, then changed the subject abruptly.

'Come along. You must be dying for a bath and a nap before lunch. You're in the bedroom you girls shared as kids. Jade will have the guest-suite when she arrives.'

'When will that be?'

Rhoda looked away. 'Oh, there's no tearing hurry after all. The wedding is not for another few days. I arranged for them not to be rushed into the nupitals without catching their breaths so to speak.'

'Hardly a rush,' Tina said. 'Didn't you say in your letter to me that they've known each other for quite a while in London, and then again for a bit in New York?'

'Of course they have. I thought you knew this.'

Tina, unpacking her case, said, 'Well, Jade and I haven't actually been bosom companions in latter years. We've gone very much our own ways, phoned each other occasionally, met for a meal. But not even that for at least a year, and since she went off to America we've lost touch even more, unfortunately.'

'She is such a busy little girl,' Rhoda said fondly.

Tina looked up. 'And so am I.'

After her bath Tina dozed off and overslept. When she hurriedly dressed and went out to the stoep, Rhoda and Scott were there having drinks.

'Sleepy-head!' scolded Rhoda acidly. 'You're holding us up. Didn't you get any sleep at all on the plane?'

Scott coughed discreetly and, meeting his eyes, Tina felt her colour rising. Plain to see in his teasing glance was the memory of her head on his shoulder, and then his glance lengthened into a holding of her eyes in a way that deliberately recalled the kiss that had passed between them a few hours ago. It was sheer wickedness on his part to remind her of it, she felt, and decided to retaliate in kind, saying with a sweet insincere smile: 'My future brother-in-law knows how well I slept on the plane. He made me most comfortable!'

Scott laughed and Rhoda looked suspiciously from him to Tina, but nothing more was said on the subject.

After lunch, when Rhoda was about to retire for her customary nap, Tina asked if she could have the car for a drive into the countryside. The answer from Rhoda was, 'No, it wouldn't be safe for you to go wandering off on your own. There are still skellums and terrs lurking about out there.'

Scott rapped out, 'I'll drive you. Come on.' It sounded more of a command than an offer.

'Don't bother,' Tina said. 'I won't go off the beaten track.'

Ignoring her protest he took her by the

arm and hustled her into the car like some tedious brat who had got on his nerves, she thought resentfully. They drove in cool silence for a while, almost the way it had been between them in the plane. Tina judged it wise to be on guard with the man in his present mood. Obviously Jade's absence had played havoc with his pride, and she had no intention of being used as a vent for his emotions. On the other hand, a display of sympathy and commiseration from her might be misconstrued, perhaps even get out of hand, as that kiss at the airport had done earlier.

After another mile or two Scott threw her a look. 'Got your bearings yet? Know where you are?'

Tina made a wild guess: 'The Lomagundi Road?'

'Wrong.' He swung the car on to a dirt road consisting of two parallel strips of tarmac laid on a raised surface leading off into the bundu.

'This was where I was brought as a lad for my driving test,' Scott informed her, narrowing his eyes suddenly at a cloud of approaching dust raised by an oncoming car.

Tina saw it and tensed apprehensively. 'What happens now?'

'Surely you know,' was his reply as he

swung the car to the left. The next minute their vehicle lurched to a cant over the embankment and proceeded at speed using only one strip of tar while the oncoming car sped past on the remaining strip. Another lurch, getting back on the strips, threw Tina against Scott who gave her a grin. 'Thought I'd ditched us, did you? Here, why don't you have a go yourself?'

Not for anything would she have refused his mocking challenge to drive on those strips. They changed places and no sooner had she moved off than another advancing column of dust came in sight. Tina steeled herself, pressed down on the accelerator and hoped for the best as she swerved off the left-hand strip of tar and drove the tilting car at a steady speed ahead, grateful for the feel of Scott's arm behind her shoulders, his other arm poised to grab the wheel in case of need. She heard rather than saw the other car rush past in its dust, and then it was over. 'I've done it!' she sang out jubilantly.

Scott's cheek touched hers warmly for a moment. 'Well done! That was a damn good first try.'

His praise was sweet to her ears but she made light of it with a swagger: 'Pouff! there was nothing to it after all.'

Scott said something she didn't catch.

Glancing quickly at him sidelong, she caught a look in his eyes that made her heart race. It raced even faster when he said, 'Turn right there where the tar widens at the crossing,' and placed his hand over hers on the wheel, telling her to stop when she had made the turn down a narrow lane running between a riot of flowers on either side.

'Remember the cosmos, Tina, and how they grow wild here at this time of year?' He leant across her to switch off the engine. 'Let's stretch our legs.'

'Oh, the wild cosmos!' she cried out and scrambled from the car to stand beside him there amongst the crowded heads of flowers in that total, primitive silence, the carpet of blooms spreading all round them.

Hand in hand, he began walking her along a stretch of grassland, the scent of the flowers bearing down on them on a warm evening breeze.

Tina looked around. 'Where are we?'

'Leopard Farm mean nothing to you?' Scott gazed down at her gently.

The name came back to her with a jolt, arousing in her sadness and sympathy as she gazed up at Scott, shading her eyes against the sun.

'It was my family home,' he said.

She looked down and said, 'Yes, Scott. I

remember now.'

He gave her hand a brief squeeze. 'We were all quite young when we had those picnics here, when you and Jade and other kids were brought along at weekends.'

She looked up at him. 'I don't remember you at all.'

'What *do* you remember?'

'A cave, with bushman paintings, and prickly pears growing nearby. They were so good to eat. And wasn't there a tank where boys sailed boats and swam?'

'Right,' he grinned. 'I once had to pull you out of the tank when you slipped off the tyre you had been floating on.'

'You lie!' she accused laughingly.

'No, cross my heart.' He gave her fingers a squeeze. 'The nipper you were then wouldn't remember being saved by a twelve-year-old hero. I recall how you screeched your head off, and very nearly mine as well.'

'I apologise,' she swept a laughing glance at him.

'Forgiven.'

The sun was hot as they climbed a slope which brought them to an outcrop of rocks, in one of which was a narrow opening. 'Here's your bushman cave,' Scott said and stood back for her to enter.

The cave was dark after the sunlight

outside, but moments later sufficient day-light filtered in to reveal the primitive art on its walls, depicting hunting figures with bows and arrows in pursuit of deer-like creatures. Tina gazed at the drawings, slowly recalling the strange atavistic fear she had felt for these pictures as a child, and was still awed by their centuries-old survival when the artists had long since become an extinct race. She shivered, imagining their spirits around her in the dim cave.

Scott's arm went protectively round her shoulders. 'You feel the little men watching you?'

'I always did. Very silly of me.'

'Well, after all, this isn't the Natural History Museum in Kensington,' he said, drawing her out into the sunshine again. They stood together surveying the sweep of mauve, pink and white cosmos stretching in thick profusion across the vlei, the sky above them a translucent shade of blue, the air sparkling — fresh and perfumed. Away in the background could be glimpsed, amongst trees, the farmhouse, long, low and white. Empty now.

'Had you lived here long?' Tina asked of Scott.

'Until I went away to study in England. After the upheaval began.'

'Your people —', she began, then bit her lip, but he continued for her.

'My mother stayed on to run the place when my father joined "Dad's Army" as it was called.' Scott broke off abruptly, his jaw developing a grim set. Tina was furious with herself for thoughtlessly asking the wrong questions. The tragedy about Scott's parents was not too clear in her mind. There had been so many like it while she safely did algebra and played games at an English boarding-school.

'My parents were both killed,' Scott said abruptly. 'Both by terrorists, and the past too is dead. I came back and did a bit of fighting and discovered there is no such thing as vengeance. So I returned to the art of making money overseas.'

'How?' Tina boldly asked.

Scott gave her a crooked smile. 'By enterprise, darling. And quite a bit of hard work, keeping several irons in the fire all going successfully.' His voice had developed a brisk, metallic quality.

'You mean your enterprises are many and varied?' she persisted.

'Anything that interests me and seems likely to yield good returns. But you're certainly an inquisitive little girl these days.

Or are you genuinely interested in me as a man?'

She turned a level gaze to meet his quizzical grey eyes. 'As a future brother-in-law,' she said coolly.

The thought of Jade immediately took shape between them, causing tension to develop. Scott glanced at his watch and said they'd better be getting back. On the way home silence came down on them again, with a feeling of tension. Tina, under her lashes, cast secret glances at the man beside her, so grim and withdrawn once again, and she wondered what a man like Scott Kyle could possibly have found in common with her frivolous and sparkling step-sister.

THREE

The moment they arrived back home Rhoda pounced on them with a welter of words, directed mainly at Scott:

'I'm just furious with myself for not stopping you from going out! Oh dear me, you'll never guess what happened.' She wrung her hands. 'Jade phoned you, Scott. From America, you know. She was bitterly disappointed to hear that you were not home. I really feel you should have stayed in.'

Scott took a deep breath and promptly offered to book a return call at once.

'No, no! Jade will call again. You see, it appears she has been swept away into some very urgent and important work. Shooting a movie, I think she said. Wonderful, isn't it?' Rhoda's tone softened and her hand moved upwards to his shoulder as she began to cajole. 'We must try to understand, dear. We must be very, very patient, mustn't we?'

Scott shrugged himself out of reach. 'I'll

call her anyway.'

Rhoda scurried after him in strange alarm. 'No! Wait, Scott, wait! Jade didn't leave a number to call.'

This new light on the matter caused a somehow threatening silence during which Scott slowly turned and fixed on his future mother-in-law a look icy enough to shrivel the grass, Tina thought. Then, with a curt 'Excuse me,' he turned and strode off indoors.

Rhoda released her pent-up breath and turned to Tina for support:

'Why should he be so angry? Can Jade help being popular? She is ruled by the demands of her career, which is flourishing sky-high. Fame and fortune are at stake you know, Tina.'

'Not to mention her marriage,' Tina murmured, but at that moment Rhoda, glancing at her watch, gasped: 'Look at the time! I must rush off to meet Gerrit at the airport. He detests being kept waiting!'

On her way out to the car Rhoda glanced back and said: 'And you, Tina, since you're the cause of Scott missing Jade's call, it's up to you to calm him down.'

Tina thoughtfully made her way to her room, feeling dispirited and decidedly limp after the crisis, which Rhoda somehow managed to blame on her. And Scott's face had been like thunder. Accusingly?

She flopped down on the window-seat where Matches brought her a tray of tea. Her blank gaze out of the window came to sudden focus on the swimming-pool glittering under the sun like a blue gem set in an expanse of green lawn. Accepting its enticement she quickly changed into her swimsuit, grabbed a towel from the bathroom and ran out barefoot to take a running plunge into the water. Then, refreshed and calmed, she stretched out on to the float to soak up the westering sun.

A stiffening breeze nudged the lilo haphazardly along the pool while Tina lay on it serene and sublimely relaxed, but not for long. All at once there was a 'plop' as something cold and rubbery landed on her bare midriff, and when her startled glance encountered the bulging eyes of a small green frog staring back at her, she let out a shrill scream of horror. The frog took off in a flash, but the next minute Tina herself was down in the water, leaving the capsized float shuddering above her.

A few submerged moments later she felt herself gripped and lifted up in a pair of strong, muscular arms. She and her resucer remained for a few moments treading water, pressed close together while he brushed the wet hair off her face. When she made efforts to free herself, Scott continued to hold her, scowling down at her. 'Confound it!' he said. 'You gave me a fright. I don't think I've ever moved so fast in my life. Thought you'd gone and fainted down there.'

'Sorry,' she murmured.

'And all because of a harmless little frog! I saw the whole performance on my way out here. What the blazes kept you down so long?' he demanded.

'Shock,' she snapped. 'I loathe frogs landing on my stomach.' Tina plunged away from him and swam fast towards the surrounding patio, followed more leisurely by Scott.

She lay back on the tiles for a few moments, recovering herself, while Scott stood over her. 'One thing's for sure,' he said. 'You certainly haven't lost the knack of screaming like hell, although several other things have changed for the better since I last pulled you out of the drink.' His twinkling glance swept over her.

Tina sat up abruptly and reached for her towel. Scott got to it first and helped wrap it round her. 'What I meant,' he said, 'was how well you have learned to swim. Unfortunately, you seem no more grateful for being saved now than you were that first time.'

'Perhaps because I haven't been saved.'

'Didn't I just rescue you from that fierce old frog?'

'If it pleases you to be funny,' she said, dabbing her hair with one end of the enormous bath towel. At that moment Matches came out to the patio and said, 'Madam just phoned.'

'Why?' asked Scott casually.

'She say Master's plane delayed one hour. Madam must wait at airport.'

'Good,' said Scott happily, and Matches departed.

The sun sank expeditiously, as usual in those parts, leaving a brief spell of twilight during which the pair at the pool lingered awhile, becoming part of the mystic silence which not even a bird dared break. The subject of Jade went unmentioned. Which only seemed to add to the peace.

Tina reluctantly broke the spell. 'Oh well,' she sighed, rising to her feet. 'I suppose it's time to dress up for meeting my stepmother's husband.' And then, suppressing a giggle, 'Oh! That didn't come out right, did it?'

Scott got up and encircled her shoulders with his arm. 'Not important,' he chuckled, conducting her indoors. 'There's time anyway for us to enjoy a quiet drink together before they get here,' he had just finished saying when two cars came swinging through the gateway and braked alongside the verandah steps. A total of seven people got out, all of them young and two of them black. 'Anyone home?' they chorused.

Scott, perfectly at ease, and dignified in his swimming-trunks, went out to meet them politely. 'Hello,' he said, and introduced himself.

The first of the arrivals up the steps advanced with outstretched hand. 'Mike Hatton. And you must be Jade's fiancé?'

'Right,' said Scott flatly.

Everyone shook hands with him and said, 'Congratulations.'

The one named Mike Hatton fixed his eyes keenly on Tina who was standing by self-effacingly in her towel. 'And this is — ?' He held out his hand to her.

'Jade's sister,' she told him.

Everyone gathered round to shake her by the hand, while Mike Hatton explained to Scott that they had come at Rhoda's invitation for a party — a reunion party of old friends. 'We young die-hards are alleged to have all grown up here together.'

Above their heads Tina's eyes telegraphed to Scott a frantic question: A party! Had

Rhoda forgotten?

Scott returned a bland smile and calmly led the guests indoors while Tina fled to slip on a wrap and rush to the kitchen. There she found Matches, unperturbed, leisurely decorating a trifle and at the same time listening to a portable radio at his elbow.

'Did Madam tell you about a party this evening?' Tina breathlessly demanded.

Matches gave her a slow grin. 'Uh-huh. Surprise party. Is nothing. Just some barbecue out backside. Everything quite ready, come see.' He padded with her outdoors to where, in the back garden, a charcoal roasting-fire glowed brilliantly in a large metal drum halved lengthwise. On a table beside it was arrayed the as yet uncooked feast of steaks, kebabs on sticks, boerewors sausage by the yard and a selection of fresh salads in cut glass bowls. Matches said that bread rolls were keeping hot in the kitchen. 'And beer keeping cold in fridge,' he added knowingly.

Beef and beer, Tina recalled hearing, were at least two commodities of which Zimbabwe had no shortage so far. She left Matches to his unruffled efficiency and went to dress herself in jeans and cotton shirt.

Rejoining the guests later, she found that

Scott, dressed in bush jacket and slacks — presumably for old times' sake — had them all clustered round a small bar rigged up in the spare garage. Seeing her enter he saluted her with his raised tankard and winked a signal that things were under control, and being enjoyed.

At that same moment Rhoda heralded her arrival from the doorway, while behind her back Gerrit van Tonder slipped in on tiptoe like a latecomer to an important lecture; and actually Rhoda was showing every sign of being about to deliver a speech.

She clapped her hands for attention: 'Hello, everybody. I just have a few words to say.'

The hubbub tailed off reluctantly in response to that high, imperious voice.

Rhoda waited for total silence before continuing:

'My apologies for being late, dears. I just hope this little surprise reunion has been pleasant for Scott and Tina, for whom it was planned.' Rhoda smiled indulgently at both parties. 'I shall now take this opportunity of introducing them to you properly.'

'Oh, but we've all properly introduced ourselves already,' one of the black guests assured her cheerfully, but Rhoda, taking no notice, walked up to Scott and linked arms with him.

'Meet my future son-in-law, Scott Kyle, an ex-Rhodesian and a very important man these days in international business circles.'

Scott muttered something inaudible and scowled, which prompted Rhoda to hasten on. 'And now I want you all to welcome my other daughter, Tina, who is back here for the wedding. You will all remember her from your days of growing up together in our former régime. Tina is learning to be a writer in London.' Rhoda made that sound like an exceptionally mediocre achievement.

Someone began to clap enthusiastically and shout 'Bravo!' It was Mike Hatton, who was soon quelled by Rhoda's upraised hand. 'And now to the main point,' she said. 'My daughter Jade was to be here for this occasion, but unfortunately she has been delayed by the demands of her career. As you know, she has risen to dizzy heights in the modelling worlds of London, Paris and New York. There is a possibility of her going into films quite soon.'

'What about marriage?' someone from the back wanted to know.

'Luckily,' said Rhoda, 'Jade's future husband is extremely supportive and encouraging in regard to her aims. Dear Scott understands from his own experience how important it is to be dedicated to one's career, whether man or woman. He has done a great deal to help Jade climb the ladder of success and will continue to do so after they are married.'

Polite murmurs vibrated round the room, while Rhoda gazed searchingly around. 'And to Scott I would say . . .' But he was nowhere to be seen.

Rescuing that moment of hiatus came the voice of Rhoda's husband bellowing in sergeant-major fashion from outdoors: 'Hey, you lot in there! Come on out and let's get started!' A sudden blare of music followed his words, forcing Rhoda's voice to rise to operatic heights: 'You may all start dancing and enjoying yourselves now,' she screeched. But they had already rushed off to do just that on the patio under the stars, beside the glowing barrel of coal.

Tina held back until the rush was over, and then she noticed Scott standing by himself, silhouetted by the fire's glow. He seemed deeply absorbed in private thoughts, but despite his withdrawn air she went and stood quietly by his side.

At first he showed no sign of having noticed her presence. After a while she raised her face to the night air and ventured to say, 'This is perhaps the way I used to remember home when they first sent me away. This scent of evening flowers and woodsmoke and warm dew-drenched grass.'

Glancing at her sideways, eyebrow cocked, he said, 'And roasting sausages?'

Tina shook her head. 'No. Too unromantic.'

'Huh. How much do you really remember of the old life here?'

'Just bits and pieces.'

'Good memories?'

'I wasn't old enough to be selective between good and bad. Tonight brings me a nostalgia for how it all was on the whole.'

'It's idle to yearn for what's gone forever,' Scott said quietly.

'But has it really gone completely? Look at them.' She indicated the dancers. 'They're carrying on regardless.'

'They're carrying on,' he agreed. 'It helps to be adaptive.'

'I'm glad it's not worse for the stayers-on,' she said.

Scott threw her a quick look. 'Did you expect it to be? Did you care?'

'Sort of,' she shrugged. 'But they seem to be managing all right. Perhaps people always do, when they have to.'

'Perhaps.' Scott took her by the hand and

led her into the crowd of dancers. 'Come on, let's show the flag.'

'Which one?' she giggled.

'Whichever. A flag is a flag.' He took her in his arms and at that moment it was as if a current of electricity passed between them, leaving them vibrating to the nearness of each other and to the slow, sentimental music. After a while, somehow — as if by accident — their cheeks touched, they drew closer and stayed so on purpose, dancing off into the moon-dappled shade of an old frangipani tree laden with strong-scented flowers.

'Romantic enough for you?' Scott breathed, almost against her lips.

'Far too much,' she murmured in reply, a potent combination of attraction and danger making her blood race. Careful, warned her sedate little inner voice! As if she didn't know! As if she couldn't cope!

FOUR

Gerrit van Tonder, having organised an outside dancing area beside the pool, had appointed himself musical director for the evening. One after another, the seductive old tunes, sung by great stars of the past, poured from his amplifier out into the moonlit garden.

Tina had been unable to avoid yet another dance with Scott, although now her confidence in being able to hold her own while held close in his arms was rapidly diminishing. For one thing, the warm heady night, perfumed with flowers, was having a stimulating effect on the pleasurable chemistry already flourishing between herself and her step-sister's fiancé. Added to this was the knightly way Scott had of cherishing her close against himself as they moved sensuously to those beguiling old rhythms of the past:

. . . Gonna take a sentimental journey
A sentimental journey home

Scott spoke softly against her cheek: 'D'you think Gerrit meant this one specially for us nostalgic expatriates?'

Tina, dancing with eyes shut, replied at last: 'I think it was meant for you and Jade dancing together after the wedding, perhaps.'

Nothing more was said for a while and the disc was changed to:

Love me tender, love me true
All my dreams fulfil

Tina felt Scott's arms tighten around her a little. 'You really ought to dance with someone else now,' she hastily suggested.

'Why?' he demanded.

'Just to be sociable. They're all here in honour of you and Jade.'

'That so? Well, since Jade isn't here, I'd rather be told more about you. Where d'you live in London?'

'South Kensington.'

'Alone?'

'Um.'

'I'm glad.'

She looked up and asked why it gladdened him.

47

Scott' reply was gruff: 'That's not a question I can answer truthfully, at this moment. Not even to myself — certainly not in my present state of mind.'

'I do understand how frustrating it must be for you —' she began, but Scott quickly danced her off further into the frangipani tree until it formed a wide canopy above their heads. There he stopped to gaze deeply into her moonlit eyes.

'I doubt if you can, Tina.'

His lips brushed her mouth as he spoke, and Tina frantically tried to break from his arms and run, but it was too late. With a soft, desperate-sounding exclamation Scott crushed her hard against himself, covering her mouth with his lips in a kiss that instantly set her blood on fire, while Gerrit, the music-maker, unwittingly added fuel of his own:

Darling, je vous aime beaucoup
Je ne sais pas what to do
Vous avez completely stolen my heart

Tina slowly abandoned herself to the rapture of that kiss, heedless of consequences, feeling at the back of her mind that nothing really depended on this stray moment of magic which stood by itself in eternity, a spark of exquisite experience that soon would pass and be forgotten. Their lips clung hungrily, in goodbye, she thought, because surely such stolen joy could not last much longer.

She was right. The dream was shattered suddenly by an announcement that Scott was wanted on the telephone. That would be Jade's promised call, of course, Tina realised, falling to earth.

The instant Scott's arms slackened round her she pushed him roughly away and fled to her room where she had to sit down abruptly because of the turmoil of emotion tearing her apart.

It was some time before she noticed that the white, huge-eyed face she was staring at was her own reflection in the dressing-table mirror. Glaring at it in sudden anger she snatched off her ear-rings, unbuttoned her blouse, shrugged off her bra, all in great fury.

'Sucker!' she flung at the mirror. 'Keeping Jade's fiancé warm for her is *not* why you're here!' (A reference to times in childhood when out of kindness she had kept Jade's bed warm in winter.)

The rage she felt was directed against herself for a lowering of defences, a naïve over-reaction that was quite against her nature. She thought of Scott, reassured and happy now, talking to his love on the phone, all else forgotten. As it certainly should be! Glancing at the mirror, Tina was astonished to see that her eyes were bright with tears. She brushed them roughly aside. 'Fool!'

Inevitably, Gerrit sent over his own contribution to the moment:

When a lovely flame dies
Smoke gets in your eyes

Tina got up and shut the window with a bang before flinging herself into bed, exhausted by her unusual outburst.

Almost immediately Rhoda came swishing into the room with barely a knock. She plumped herself down at the foot of Tina's bed. 'What's wrong? I saw you rush off in a great hurry.'

'I have a bad headache,' Tina said truthfully.

'Dear me, how sudden.'

'And I'd like to rest if you wouldn't mind.'

Rhoda shook her head. 'Don't lie to me, Tina. I'm not here to scold, but I must say your open flirting with Scott was in shocking bad taste.'

'Shouldn't you be saying the same thing to Scott?' Tina's colour rose.

50

'Oh, I know he isn't blameless in the matter,' Rhoda grudgingly admitted. 'But the man is missing his fiancée, he's in a state of frustration and therefore vulnerable.'

'Oh, well, don't worry,' Tina said tersely. 'He's been speaking to Jade on the phone and must be feeling just fine again. Soon they'll be married, and all will be well.' She leant back against the pillows and closed her eyes. 'May I have an aspirin, please?'

Ignoring the request, her stepmother blurted: 'He was *not* on the phone to Jade. The call he took was a local one from one of his business associates here in Harare.'

Tina's eyelashes fluttered but she kept them lowered as Rhoda continued:

'Now listen to me, my girl. This isn't London. We all know the morals of the English.'

'Do you?'

'Well, no offence, but in a closed community like ours out here, indiscreet behaviour becomes magnified and scandal so easily rages. I'm sure your behaviour with Scott must have been noticed tonight.'

'I promise to ignore Jade's fiancé in future. Won't talk to him, if you like. Give him a wide berth,' Tina offered.

'You needn't be sarcastic,' Rhoda snapped. 'Let me inform you that women find Scott very attractive. Jade's going to have her hands full coping with that problem after marriage. I don't want her to face it before time.'

Tina's lack of comment angered her stepmother. 'I daresay you're feeling flattered by Scott's attentions, but let me warn you, Tina, it means nothing, coming from him. Nothing! He has a reputation for playing the field, although his intentions towards Jade have always been honourable, make no mistake. Scott is utterly devoted to my daughter.'

Tina raised her eyes and asked quietly: 'Then what are you afraid of?'

Rhoda, choosing not to hear, went on quickly: 'I've hoped all along for one of you girls to marry into the Kyle family, and so it was just wonderful when Scott asked Jade, especially after he became —' she paused.

'Rich and successful?' Tina offered.

'All right then. I'm not ashamed of rejoicing for Jade's sake that her future husband will be able to indulge her extravagant nature.'

'I'm happy for her too,' Tina said truthfully, and it turned out to be the right remark.

Rhoda at once burst into warm loving smiles and patting motherly hands: 'You're a really good girl, Tina. So understanding. I'm certain you'll find a fine man of your own one day.'

She rose and kissed Tina on the forehead: 'No hard feelings, now. My little talk was meant to guard you from unhappiness.'

'Very kind of you,' Tina said dully. 'But you needn't worry about me.'

Rhoda put out the light, opened the window and left.

In wafted another contribution from Gerrit:

Birds do it, bees do it
Even educated fleas do it,
Let's do it, let's fall in love.

Tina pulled the sheet over her head, wondering why she had to be falling in love for the first time with someone who was not hers to have. Someone who was merely filling in time before the arrival of his true love.

At breakfast next morning Tina was surprised to see three of the previous night's guests assembled round the table with Scott, a young married pair named Meg and Tony Young, and Mike Hatton.

Scott was on his feet, about to leave. He nodded casually to Tina, as if the frangipani episode had never taken place, and she nodded back with equal coolness before Mike touched her arm for attention and told her:

'Scott has some business up at the Vumba Mountains today and has agreed to let Tony and Meg and myself come along for a weekend. Tony and I are keen trout fishermen and Meg's along for the ride. How about you joining us, Tina?'

Tina replied with forced vivacity: 'Oh, but I'd love to!' She glanced quickly at Scott and added, 'If I'm invited?'

Scott's attitude made it clear he was against her joining the party. 'It won't be the Ritz, you know. We'll be roughing it camp-style, sleeping rough in tents for one night. And besides — I have something important to do there.'

Meg Young chipped in at once. 'Well, Tina and I can keep each other company while you men are off doing your own thing. Can't we, Tina?'

'Count me in,' said Tina, ignoring Scott's surliness.

'Great!' rejoiced Mike. 'Luckily I packed a spare tent in the van, just in case.'

Scott scowled briefly and then, with a shrug, he turned and walked away.

The five of them and one dog — Rhoda and Gerrit's Rhodesian ridgeback — set off in two vehicles, Scott driving a van packed in the rear with camping equipment. In front with him travelled Tina and Mike. The Youngs followed behind in their own car, with the dog, Simba, asleep on the back seat.

Some miles out of Harare they began the climb into fresh mountain air, and scenery that to Tina was reminiscent of Scotland, complete with silvery trout streams, ferns and bracken. Out in the distance could be seen the border into former Portuguese-governed territory. Tina understood from the men yarning beside her that they were now entering an area where fierce fighting and terrorist activities had taken place during the Rhodesian war. She found it difficult to believe that such peace and beauty had once been torn apart by explosions and gunfire.

'Thank heaven it's all over now,' she voiced fervently.

Mike Hatton contradicted her. 'Not quite over. There are stray gangs of bandits and rebels still going it on their own in some places. It's necessary to keep an eye open when off the beaten track.'

Just then Scott changed gear and slowed the van to a crawl and leant out of the window to watch for the car behind them to show up. When it made no appearance he stopped, and they all waited in tense silence as the minutes ticked by. Tina felt the unspoken word 'ambush' hanging over them.

At last Scott, apparently hearing something, started the van's engine and moved forward as the Youngs' car came round a bend, with Simba at the rear window barking like fury.

'Darned hound jumped out to chase something and we had to stop and get him back,' shouted Tony Young, driving abreast for a minute before the procession proceeded. Tina felt limp with relief, and thought she could understand why Scott hadn't wanted an amateur like herself in his party!

They arrived at a camping site chosen by Scott, situated above bushy slopes and thick undergrowth. The ground had been cleared by previous campers and now the three men set up camp and made a fire while Meg and Tina unpacked the food.

Lunch was a selection of last night's leftover meats, which they roasted on skewers, and Matches had provided salad and fruit. While the others chatted amiably, Tina noticed Scott's air of withdrawal, as if he had something troublesome on his mind.

Something perhaps to do with his coming up here, judging by the searching looks he cast about at intervals. The watchful look of a sentry?

He caught her gazing at him and his look softened.

The others were light-heartedly discussing a prevalent shortage of toothpaste in the country, or rather a shortage of tubes, so that people were having to collect the paste from factories in various domestic containers, including teacups. They made a joke of it, but Tina sensed the underlying irony.

'You can get used to anything,' Meg Young sighed, displaying inherited British stoicism to a degree that made Tina think of the grit it had taken for these ex-colonials to endure violence and loss of many kinds and yet be able to joke in the face of what fate might yet have in store. Under her lashes she stole a glance at Scott's strong, purposeful features, the firm mouth that just a few hours ago had possessed her own so passionately now seemed hard and implacable. He looked up and their eyes met and, as if reading her thoughts, he gave her a slow, cynical smile that mocked the sudden burning of her cheeks.

The others made a stir, yawning and stretching and announcing their intention to take a short siesta.

Scott was nowhere to be seen when Tina decided to set off for a stroll on her own, but she had walked only a short distance when suddenly he was there, tramping beside her.

'It's not particularly safe for you to wander off alone,' he said with a roughness that roused her to retort: 'Obviously you consider me soft and degenerate compared with the stayers-on, taking it on the chin with a smile as they are, settling for toothpaste out of a teacup!'

His laugh was hollow. 'They've settled for much less than that, actually.' His gaze strayed over the mountain scene. 'It's remarkable what people will put up with for love of a country. Not that I blame you for preferring civilisation.'

'Isn't that what you yourself prefer?' she countered. 'Was it not the reason why you left here in the first place?'

Just as it seemed he was choosing to ignore her remark, he said, quietly:

'There were several reasons, which I am not about to discuss with you now.'

Tina bit her lip, accepting the snub as only what she had asked for.

They walked on in silence for about twenty minutes before coming upon Mike and Tony, hopefully preparing to fish at the trout stream. Nearby lay Simba, jowls on paws, tied to a tree and sulking.

Scott said to Tina: 'I'm going to leave you here with them.'

'Tied to a tree?' she asked sarcastically.

'You'll be safer with them than with me,' he said, adding softly with a gleam in his eye, 'and I don't mean what you're thinking.'

'I'm thinking you're beastly rude,' she snapped, watching him stride away into the surrounding wilderness. She was amazed at her own rudeness, so foreign to her nature. Oh come on, Jade, marry him and let me escape to my life in London, she thought.

As Scott continued on without a backward glance at her, some strange form of rebellion possessed Tina; a determination not to let herself be dominated by him. She waited only long enough until he was completely lost from sight, then set off after him while the men at the stream were busy with their own affairs.

She supposed that her original intention was to follow in his tracks, and eventually to turn up back at camp, all safe and sound, to prove her capabilities. Somewhere along the line, unfortunately, she took a few wrong turnings, ending on a pathway that dwindled to a mere lane wandering between the trees where Scott's footsteps could no longer be heard. And now she was lost.

Well, not lost, she assured herself. Just temporarily off route. She sat down on a protuberance of rock, thinking it would be sensible to call out to Scott. Sensible yet undignified. Strategy, not panic, was called for, and she decided to rest awhile and get her bearings.

She had been there just a few minutes when from behind a clump of bushes crept two wild-looking characters in ragged bush-suits, which at some time in the past might have been military uniforms. The clothes were now as filthy and unkempt as the pair of creatures wearing them. Tina caught her breath at seeing they were carrying unreliable-looking and dirty rifles, while one of them also had a knife slung from his belt. Slowly, with obvious curiosity, they advanced on her across the grass, the whites of their eyes glaring starkly in their black, begrimed young faces.

Paralysed, Tina sat watching them. Her voice was the only part of her that would function: 'Go away!' she shouted. 'Buzz off! I'm not alone, you know.'

On they came regardless, like two stray

cats about to pounce on the same petrified bird.

Then Tina opened her mouth and began to scream at the top of her voice, without pause. The din she created ripped through the thicket all round like an alarm siren, which had the effect of stopping her attackers dead, with stunned looks on their faces.

She saw them gaze wildly at each other. One of them levelled his gun, aimed at her and was about to pull the trigger when his companion gave out a yell. The gun fired off into the tree overhead.

Tina sprang to her feet and bolted towards a line of trees not far off. Halfway there she heard the rifle fire again. It missed her as she continued racing for the trees. Then she saw the figure of another man running towards her — a familiar figure.

'Scott!' she shrieked. 'Get back, get back!' She ended on a sob of remorse. Her cries for help had brought him into a trap. Because of her own silly fault Scott was about to be killed!

'Darling, don't, don't!' she screamed, but he raced forward.

FIVE

Scott came running up, caught her in his arms and threw her to the ground in one continuous flow of movement, placing his body over hers. She heard him shouting with authority to the hostile pair in a language she could not understand.

The firing stopped. From where she lay, tasting dust, Tina heard footsteps shuffling forward. 'Lie still,' Scott muttered, his hand pressing down hard on the back of her neck. Even at that critical moment she resented his roughness, but as it seemed they were both about to lose their lives, she sobbed out hysterically: 'It's all my fault. Forgive me.'

'Shut up!' he said.

By twisting her head sideways Tina could see what happened next. The two enemies had come to a halt with their feet just inches from her face, one pair unshod, the other wearing tattered army boots.

Scott relaxed his grip on her neck and stood up, shielding her still with his body. She heard him rap out one single word that sounded like a name she vaguely remembered: 'Cheeza!'

The bare feet gave a short backward leap and the owner of them exclaimed something sharply in his own dialect.

Scott fired a volley of words in the same language, and in return received a wild shout. To Tina it sounded like exultation. She shut her eyes tightly and held her breath, expecting the worst, her heart beating like an African drum.

Scott next spoke in English, for her benefit, she imagined:

'You were a clever boy once, Cheeza, and now you're a bandit. Why?'

The barefoot one rubbed his stomach with the palm of one hand. 'Hungry.'

'Aren't your bosses paying you?'

Cheeza shook his head, dejected and angry-looking. 'Long time no pay.'

'Then you're stupid not to quit and go find yourself a job in town.'

The man replied: 'You my long-time brudder. Always I listen to you, but play-brudder only. Now no more play but fight. Now my father, your father dead. Me enemy. You want to kill me?'

'No!' shouted Scott angrily. 'I'm here because you sent a message to meet you here. Is it true you're sick of banditry and want to come back, Cheeza?'

'Is true. But I got nowhere to go, no job. Nothing.'

'I'm still your friend,' Scott spoke gently. 'I can fix up work for you in Harare, and a kia to live in. Do you really want to come?'

Tina tentatively raised herself on her elbows and watched the scene.

Cheeza said to Scott, while pointing to his companion: 'He my blood-brudder. You got some money for us?'

'Maybe,' Scott replied warily. 'Maybe I'll give you money to go home and buy seeds for planting food, not bullets for killing friends.'

Delving into his pockets he emptied them, letting the money fall through his fingers to the ground. The pair immediately pounced on it, dividing, scooping up.

Scott held the back of Cheeza's collar and urged him to his feet. They gazed at one another, eye-to-eye. 'Understand, Cheeza. Explain to your comrade that this is not ter-rorist pay.'

'Him my piccanin blood-brudder,' Cheeza repeated.

'Okay, so teach him what's good for you

both. And after your planting is done at home, come and see Matches in Harare. He will tell you where I've arranged a job for you. I'll be going away again soon.'

Scott made some further crisp remarks in the vernacular, which caused Cheeza to execute a ragged salute before diving off into the undergrowth with his companion.

When they were gone, Tina stood up and asked shakily: 'What was that last thing you said?'

Scott gazed down at her grimly. 'Putting it politely, I said the next time they might not be so lucky.' He pulled an ironic face. 'It should be the other way round, of course. If Cheeza's dad hadn't worked on my own father's farm, if I hadn't spoilt him a bit as a kid because of the way he followed me round like a lost puppy, Cheeza might not have sent me this message via the grapevine that he needed my help. I intended meeting him alone here, but your intrusion at a critical moment . . .'

'I'm sorry,' she said miserably. 'You saved my life, Scott.'

'A pleasure,' he said drily, turning away and trudging her back towards camp without speaking again.

Tina, still shaken by the episode, saw from Scott's manner that he was displeased with her for complicating a dangerous and touchy situation which might so easily have blown up, even without her appearance on the scene. She began to regard Scott as a man of rare stature, capable of risking his own life to help a friend. A dubious friend at that — a terrorist!

'I suppose it remains to be seen whether Cheeza will repay your kindness,' she ventured to say.

'There's always a chance he won't,' Scott said. 'But the effort had to be made. Don't mention this affair to the others, will you?'

'No.' She shook her head, warmed and flattered by his trust.

'And, of course, no little freelance piece to the papers back home?'

'Of course not,' she said meekly.

As the sun dipped low and shadows began to gather, Scott took her hand to hurry her along; a simple enough gesture of friendly concern, although in her emotionally over-wrought state Tina read more into it than seemed sensible. The feel of his hand was warm and secure and possessive.

When they arrived back in camp the others were gathered round a newly-kindled fire, drinking beer, except for Meg who was to one side, threading chops and slices of tomato on a skewer. She glanced up as Tina joined her. 'Everything's ready to eat in a while. Let's go join the boys for a drink.' Her glance sharpened on Tina. 'You all right?'

'Yes. Why?'

'You're so breathless, and your eyes are glowing fever-bright.'

Tina lowered her lashes. 'I've been walking rather fast.'

'Uh-huh?' Meg raised her eyebrows with a smile.

There was no lack of cheer round the fire that evening and no tension. Tina, glancing at Scott and remembering the secret they were keeping from the others, felt that the danger they had shared together had somehow forged a bond between them. It was something to cherish, she thought, calling herself a fool for thinking along such lines. She hoped Scott would never guess how she felt about him.

The pure mountain air made them all sleepy enough to retire early. When Tina lay snuggled in her sleeping-bag, watching the starlit sky through the open tent flap, Scott brought the ridgeback to her and tethered him to a peg.

'You needn't feel nervous with Simba here to guard you,' he said, bending to smooth back her hair as if she were a child. 'Remember that Simba means lion, and this is a lion-hearted breed. But for heaven's sake don't let him off the leash or he'll be off after wildlife.'

As she murmured her thanks, Scott took her hand and squeezed it, making her breath come faster. And then he placed his lips to her forehead. 'You've had a hard time today, little one.'

Tina struggled against a longing to slip her arms round his neck and draw down his lips to hers. Then suddenly he was gone.

Through the open tent-flap she lay watching Scott by the fire, sitting elbows on knees, face turned to gaze across the hills. Keeping watch, she thought; or was he thinking yearningly about Jade, allowing his longing for her to surface now that he imagined himself alone and unobserved?

Tina could sense his loneliness and had to control her own burning impulse to go out and keep him company, encourage him to talk out his feelings for Jade with her. But, of course, that would never do.

She watched him until her eyelids closed. It seemed only a few moments later that she opened them again with a sense of something being amiss. True, Scott was gone from the fireside. Gone also was the dog. 'Simba!' she called hoarsely. 'Hey,

Simba!' But she found herself addressing just his collar and leash.

Drawing herself out of bed she went out to look around. Everything was still and silent. She could imagine Scott being furious with her for allowing Simba to escape. Where on earth was the dog? She softly called it again and there was a sudden scurry some yards ahead in the shrubs.

Tina hastily donned a woolly over the track-suit she'd been sleeping in and went in search of the missing animal, or rather after the vague sounds she was following in the bushes, like something being dragged.

The pursuit lasted rather too long and she was tempted to give up, except that Scott would hold her responsible for the dog, seeing that he had particularly asked her not to let it escape.

It occurred to her at last that she might have been following a false trail. And now, of course, she was lost! Out here in the dark. Scott would be livid if he knew! 'If I live to tell the tale,' she muttered, setting out to follow the course of the stream which had appeared, as if from nowhere, at her feet.

A strange, mysterious light now came through to help her along. Not so mysterious, she discovered in a few minutes when, emerging from the thicket, she saw that it was early dawn. Apparently she had dozed off for most of the night, and there ahead of her now was a fisherman angling for trout. The dog that sat statue-still on the banks of the stream was none other than Simba, with his eyes fixed on Scott, the pair of them apparently unaware of her arrival.

Tina was about to slip away quietly, when Scott suddenly turned his head and saw her. He waved. She waved back in relief. He held up a couple of trout and smiled, apparently taking her dishevelled appearance on the scene for granted. And not a word about the dog as he gathered up his things and joined her, casually placing an arm round her shoulders to lead her away.

'The other chaps can catch their own breakfast. These two will do for us. Let's get back.'

Faces raised to the cool, fresh air, they made their way companionably back to camp. Tina could not leave well alone; she just had to know why Scott was not scolding her.

'When d'you start giving me heck about the dog? For letting him escape?'

Scott looked at her and laughed, and squeezed her by the shoulders against himself. 'You did no such thing. I came and let him loose for a run at five-thirty. He

behaved very well, I thought.' He looked
down at her with a smile. 'You were sleeping like a babe, as you did that night on the
aircraft. It seemed a shame to disturb you.'

Disturb her! As if he hadn't done that
already in a way that made her wish she had
never come back for Jade's wedding. Made
her wish for more maturity to cope with a
situation which Jade was prolonging by her
continued absence.

Then and there she resolved to keep
herself at arm's length from Scott Kyle,
even if it meant being downright rude.

Six

After breakfasting on trout, the campers set out to visit one of the most popular hotels of that area, whose manager had been a school-friend of Scott's. The place was known to have gone down as a result of the war and in fact no one knew whether it was still functioning, but they were eager to find out.

About half an hour's hike brought them to the now rather neglected-looking colonial-style building set in imposing grounds spread around it like the skirts of some grande dame of earlier times. Rather ragged skirts now.

Speaking in hushed voices they entered the main entrance hall, and finding it deserted, passed through to a large wood-panelled bar-lounge. Here it was as if ghosts of the past inhabited the place in relics such as faded photographs hung on the walls, along with caricatures of bygone personalities, and also moth-eaten animal trophies of the hunter's rifle. Tina felt a shudder down her spine.

On the curved bar-counter was a bell which Scott thumped experimentally. At once a white-uniformed African bartender appeared, grinning widely at their surprise at seeing him, as if a figure in Madame Tussaud's had suddenly come alive.

They gathered round to order beers, and were again surprised when the order was promptly served. The bartender, when drawn into conversation, informed them that there was to be an official convention at the hotel the following week and things were in readiness for it.

Meg pulled a face. 'Ugh! A dull old convention. I've been told that this place used to be heaven for honeymooners, and can you wonder?' She waved to the scene outside the French windows: 'All this beauty and peace and quiet.' With a laugh she turned to her husband: 'Tony, will you promise to bring me here for our first anniversary?'

Tony grinned, flashing a glance at Scott, and said, 'Sure. But it seems another couple we all know will beat us to it in a few days.

Scott caught Tina's eyes for a moment before she quickly looked away, feeling a shaft of misery go through her. But at least her defences were up again and on no account would she let Scott demolish them.

A diversion was caused right then by the boisterous arrival of Simba who had wandered off en route and was now beside himself with excitement at having tracked down his party.

'Sorry, no dogs allowed,' the barman said, and Tina gratefully slipped off her high stool, offering to take the dog for a stroll. Seizing Simba's collar she dragged him out. Behind her she heard Scott say, 'Mind you keep to the grounds, Tina.' But her one thought at that moment was to get away from him. And his honeymoon hotel!

Walking alone seemed to clear her mind, and she was some distance away from the hotel when she wondered why Scott had undertaken this trip to the mountains at a time when Jade had promised to phone again — or had she done so already? Perhaps during the night or early morning? If so, Scott knew now the date of the wedding and was here perhaps to arrange the honeymoon. Tina could only hope this was true and that the wedding would take place very soon, allowing her to escape to London and her work as soon as possible. There she could forget the madness that had come with being in this country, which was home to her no longer but a place she badly needed to forget.

Her attention was brought back to the present. That darned dog! Simba was off, scrambling up a steep incline, dislodging small rocks into her path as she tried to follow, shouting for him to 'Heel'. He ignored her calls.

Footsteps came up behind her. It would be Mike Hatton, she felt. He had stayed close to her throughout the hike, but at this moment she was in no particular need of his company.

Then she heard the command. 'Hi, there! Wait a minute!' Scott's voice.

Tina caught her breath but continued climbing the incline after Simba, who had by now vanished over the top.

Scott's hands gripped her from behind. 'Didn't you hear, or are you bent on taking risks?'

She turned on him angrily. 'Why don't you leave me alone, Scott! I'm not the kind you take me for.'

'What kind would that be?' He gave her a little shake.

'The kind I'm told you enjoy playing around with. And now please go.'

'I came to take you back. We're leaving at once.'

'There's Simba for me to find.'

'There *was* Simba,' he said. 'You haven't a hope of controlling that dog. Allow me to get him.'

Tina was struggling to free herself of his hands when the shale underfoot collapsed, causing a minature landslide that made her lose her balance. She twisted her knee, gave a cry of pain and cannoned downwards into Scott, all at the same time. He steadied her in his arms, but the ground beneath them gave way further and they ended face to face precariously trying to stay upright. Any move Tina made to extricate herself only tangled them together more helplessly.

She felt foolish, clinging to Scott like a novice skier, arms desperately thrown round his neck, legs comically crossed and out of control.

'This,' he remarked drily, 'is literally being thrown together by fate.'

Simba chose that moment to peer down at them over the ridge. Then, barking derisively, he came tobogganing down on his four paws to fling himself at the locked couple, yelping with excitement. Under his onslaught they toppled backwards, locked in each other's arms, Tina on top of Scott,

Simba in a frenzy of delight, licking their faces and tumbling with them to the bottom of the slope.

It took a while for man, woman and dog to separate. Scott got to his feet first and helped Tina up. They stared wildly at one another for a moment and then burst out laughing. Scott quickly sobered and, taking her by the arm, steadied Tina. 'Are you hurt?' He gazed anxiously down into her eyes.

'Just a bit scraped. It's nothing,' she said, drawing away from him but he took her arm again, leading her slowly away.

They came to a field of red, yellow and white flowers. Scott bent and picked a bouquet for Tina, telling her they were Rhodesian flame lilies. 'They're strictly veld flowers, never been known to grow in gardens, but will keep in vases,' he said, as she took them from him.

Tina lightly pressed her cheek to the offering. 'How lovely they are.'

'And rare,' Scott added, gazing down at her. 'The way some women are rare.' Their eyes met for a second before he tucked her free hand under his arm and walked on in the direction from which a car's hooter sounded urgently.

'By the way,' Scott asked, 'do you really

believe I'm given to playing around with women?'

'I'm sorry I said that,' she murmured, turning pink. 'But that doesn't mean we should continue giving people cause to gossip.'

'Who said we were?'

Tina made no reply and Scott said, 'Oh, I see. Rhoda's been reading you sermons.'

Rhoda did not come out to greet them on arrival back home and Tina, sensing that her stepmother was in one of her moods, went straight to her own room and lay on the bed. The others had gone their own separate ways, and Scott had made straight for the telephone, presumably to call Jade.

Lying on the bed, her eyes shut, Tina could hear him impatiently rattling the instrument and talking loudly before banging down the receiver. Somehow he had never struck her as the banging-down type, so evidently a combination of the local telephone system and his personal worries were getting to him.

Nervous seizures seemed in vogue, Tina discovered, waking from a doze to the sound of Rhoda's voice from the stoep, declaiming in high key and not in the Shona language (which might have indicated that the garden boy, Phineas, was being scolded) but in English.

'I really do think you're being *most unreasonable,* Scott! Give the poor girl a chance, will you? Think of what Jade must be feeling, torn in two directions, or more, while all those film people rush her about, wearing her to a *frazzle!*'

'Jade's not a child!' Scott retorted sharply. 'Her choice is perfectly clear and simple. So is mine!'

'Oh, Scott, Scott. A man of the world like you must know how these things happen.'

'You bet!'

In the silence that followed, Tina could imagine Rhoda sidling up to Scott, stroking him like a cat, before continuing to say: 'Come now, dear, calm down. Jade will be here soon, like a bluebird of happiness to warm your heart again.'

The syrup in her voice made Tina cringe and wonder what Scott thought of it. Not much, she imagined.

And now Gerrit van Tonder's voice intervened: 'Well, well, here's old Scott back again. Had a nice trip, son?' His obviously forced joviality indicated a pouring of oil on troubled waters. 'Come on and have a whisky with me in the garden. Rhoda can just leave us alone there for a while.'

Tina got out of bed with a sigh of relief and went to ask Matches for a vase. He handed her a local variety consisting of a hollowed-out buffalo horn fixed horizontally to a wooden base. Back in her room Tina arranged the flame lilies along the curve of the horn, added more water and stood back to admire the effect. The flowers were so unusually lovely that she nipped off a specimen and pressed it in her diary. On some wintry day in England it would serve as a reminder of the Vumba Mountains. And Scott.

Behind her the bedroom door opened and she saw Rhoda's reflection in the mirror, watching her thoughtfully.

'I'll say you're looking very lovely,' she remarked, almost accusingly.

'Thanks.'

'Like a woman in love,' Rhoda continued, coming up to Tina and placing her hands on her step-daughter's shoulders to gaze into her eyes. 'I pray you'll find some good man of your own to make your life complete.'

'My life's just fine,' Tina said.

'You've never mentioned a boyfriend in your letters. Surely there is someone special?'

'Not a soul,' Tina smiled. 'Just a friend or

two. I like it this way.'

Rhoda sat down on the bed. 'My dear! How very different you two sisters are from each other. Even as step-sisters. There's Jade, so fond of the boys — in the very nicest way, of course. And here you are, so cool and self-sufficient, and . . .'

'Unromantic,' supplied Tina.

'I was going to say you don't take enough time off for fun, evidently. Too much seriousness, too little play. I suppose the right man will come along to claim you one day. Write and tell me as soon as that happens, won't you?'

Tina's eyes lingered on the display of flame lilies, her thoughts far from what her stepmother was saying.

Rhoda, noticing the lilies, said, 'I've tried so hard to make them grow in my garden, but those plants just go their own way. Something like you, Tina. I've always found it impossible to make you conform.'

A knock sounded on the door and Gerrit poked his head in. 'Young feller here wants to take you out, Tina.'

'Who is it?' Rhoda demanded avidly.

'That young geologist chap. Mike Hatton's the name, isn't it?'

Rhoda turned a brilliant smile on Tina. '*Such* a pleasant young man, and with excellent prospects, too. You must have made quite an impression on him, dear. Normally he's so reserved and shy.'

Tina shrugged. 'I'd rather not go out again today.'

'All right, then stay in and talk to him. It's lovely by the pool this evening. Gerrit and I will leave the pair of you alone. And do ask him to dinner.'

Tina hesitated but Gerrit cajoled, 'Come on, child, you're only young once. Give the lad a chance.'

Drinks were being dispensed on the patio when Tina went out, changed into a summery kaftan and sandals. Mike Hatton at once detached himself from a group and came to welcome her. From the corner of her eye she caught sight of Scott watching as Mike led her away into the garden.

Mike, having settled her on a garden-seat near the frangipani tree, went back to the patio and returned with two drinks. It was a dreamy evening, redolent with memories for Tina of the night Scott had kissed her in the depths of that perfumed tree.

'Penny for your thoughts,' said Mike, and she hastily pulled herself together.

'There's a show on at a night-spot called The Zambezi tonight,' Mike told her. 'I think you'd enjoy it. Will you let me take you?' His eyes lit up when Tina agreed.

'Oh, I'm delighted you've persuaded Tina to go out and have some fun,' cried Rhoda when they went to take leave. At that moment Scott rose from his chair saying he too had an appointment for the evening with his business associates, the Mukotos.

'The Mukotos!' Rhoda was impressed. They're in a very high social bracket in our new African regime, you know,' she announced all round and then turned back to Scott. 'Shall I drive you over to their place?'

'No need, Herbert Mukoto will be picking me up any minute now — in fact here he is, I believe.' A car's headlights flashed across the wall and Scott strode off with a quick 'Goodnight' and not a glance at Tina.

She sat beside Mike in his car, watching the tail-lights of the one in which Scott was being driven off. All at once she felt empty and lonely, but accepted that this was the way it was going to be until she returned to London and began to forget him.

A musical riot was rocking the walls of the Zambezi in Manica Road. Mike managed to squeeze Tina and himself into the jam of rhythm-activated bodies washed by beams of strobe lights. On a dais at one end of the room an assembly of musicians bounced about thumping drums, blowing horns, plucking strings and working a magic that kept the human puppets jerking ecstatically all round.

The beat, like the music itself, was unique, belted out on instruments among which were some weird specimens which made sounds that blended amazingly well with the conventional kind.

'You'd say it shouldn't be happening, wouldn't you?' Mike squeezed Tina's hand. 'It should be bedlam, but actually you must agree it works to make a real kind of music — though different.'

'Very different,' Tina agreed, swaying compulsively.

They stayed some time, absorbing the atmosphere, relating experimentally with the near-frenzy. Mike said the band would be going on an overseas tour soon to seek fame. The room became a thrashing sea of rhythm-inspired people and Tina felt it was time to leave. Her ears had begun to hurt.

Mike drew her away. 'Let's go. I think a drive to the top of the Koppie would clear our heads,' he told her.

'The Koppie?' she frowned, trying to remember.

They stopped in the doorway as Mike pointed to a dark hump rising behind the town. 'You've forgotten the old Koppie? It's that hill over there. Nice view from the top, of city lights,' Mike was saying when another couple came up, wanting to enter.

'Sorry,' Mike politely apologised, drawing Tina to one side as the other pair swept past, looking straight ahead, but not before Tina had recognized Scott, accompanied by a young and glamorous blonde.

She stood amazed that he should have so rudely ignored her.

'What's wrong, were you jostled?' Mike asked with concern.

'It was Scott, didn't you see?'

'No. I only have eyes for you,' he warbled idiotically, and took her away.

SEVEN

Tina took little note of where she was being driven, except that it was up a steep incline to the summit where Mike brought his car to a halt. They sat for a while gazing down silently at street lights winding out into dark Africa.

Mike broke the silence: 'I often come here on my own to think, and try to reach a decision.'

'About what?' Tina asked automatically, her thoughts wandering elsewhere.

'Well, about this job I've been offered in England, I'd like very much to go.'

'Then take the job.' Amending the abrupt sound of that, Tina added more gently, 'The experience should be valuable.'

Encouraged, he moved closer, running his arm along the backrest behind her. 'I've just about reached a decision now. And supposing I do go to England, would you let me come and see you?'

'Why not?' she said lightly and indifferently. 'I'm not often free though.'

'I suppose not,' her companion muttered glumly. 'Dozens of guys must be jostling for a date with you.'

'Oh, no,' she laughed. 'Actually I'm rather a recluse. In love with my work, so to speak.'

'Nobody works day and night.'

'I do. At least I have a good try.'

Bringing his face close to hers, Mike spoke softly. 'You'll ruin your lovely sea-green eyes.'

Tina glanced sidelong under her lashes as his arm tightened round her shoulders. 'Please look at me, Tina. You're so very lovely, but why so remote?'

She turned her head in quick surprise and his mouth was there, waiting for hers. Their lips touched and it developed into a hesitant though lingering kiss, which Tina quietly endured, waiting to discover whether her blood would catch fire, as with Scott. It did not.

Her sigh of dejection when Mike let her go prompted him to say: 'Am I boring you, ice-maiden?'

'Of course not.' She could hardly confess that another kiss, another man, had recently smashed the ice barrier round her heart and brought her close to falling in love for the first time. But with the wrong man. With her sister's man.

'How distant and uptight you are,' Mike accused ruefully. 'And there goes another of my cherished illusions. I imagined women novelists were wonderfully romantic creatures, full of warmth and fire.'

'I'm just a learner.' She forced a tight little laugh.

He squeezed her hand sympathetically. 'Not to worry. There's plenty of time.'

Mike drove her home with that awful dead feeling between them which Tina knew so well from past experience. Frustrated passion. When he brought his car to a stop in the driveway, she so pitied his disappointment that when he made a feeble attempt to kiss her again she did her best to respond with enthusiasm. It was another flop, although this time Mike had put much lingering sensuality into it, perhaps mistaking her feigned eagerness for the real thing.

She slipped hurriedly out of the car, thanked him for the evening, and ran indoors expecting never to see him again, but he pursued her in long athletic strides, caught her up on the stoep and asked, 'May I see you again? Tomorrow, perhaps?'

'I'll let you know. Goodnight.' She turned to go.

'And Tina?'

'Yes?'

In reply he touched her lips with his own and whispered, 'You're great!'

It was almost noon next day when Matches, wearing an expression of doom, awakened Tina with a tray of tea, toast and paw-paw.

She sat up quickly: 'Heavens! Look at the sun! I've badly overslept.'

'Not to worry,' Matches' voice matched his gloomy face. 'Everything upside-down today. Madam say you must please stay here. She coming talk to you now-now.'

'Why must she? What's happened?'

Matches merely raised his shoulders and departed silently. He had barely gone when Rhoda burst in.

'Oh, Tina, thank the Lord you're up!' She seemed on the edge of hysteria. 'Gerrit has gone off to work and left me to deal with this dreadful affair on my own. I feel on the verge of collapse!'

'Sit down,' Tina said, jumping up. 'Let me pour you a cup of tea. Have an aspirin as well.'

'I've aleady taken tranquillisers.' Rhoda lay back on the bed, curling her bare toes under the flowing house-coat she wore, from the pocket of which she extracted a packet of Rhodesian cigarettes, withdrew one, lit it and puffed agitatedly. Tina sat beside her, waiting.

'Scott's gone!' Rhoda blurted suddenly, causing Tina to recoil as if she'd been struck across the cheek.

'*G-gone?* Where? W-why?' she stammered, going white in the face.

'Back to London. Late last night he had a call from Jade. I think she must have begged to postpone her arrival yet again and it upset Scott. I'd no idea he could fly into such a temper or act in such an atrociously selfish way. Absolutely no thought for poor Jade's feelings. Or for mine, left with all the wedding preparations to undo.' Tears welled in Rhoda's eyes. 'You don't know how difficult things are to get in this country. I've plotted and planned trying to assemble a nice wedding for my daughter — and this is how he thanks me . . .' Loud harsh sobs ended the narrative. The sound of such anguish touched Tina's heart, and sympathy with her stepmother moved her to hug Rhoda against herself.

'There, there. Scott can't have left Harare yet. The only flight to London is tonight. Would it be all right if I went to the airport to try and reason with him to come back? He can't possibly mean the wedding to be cancelled.'

'Oh, but that's exactly what he does mean!' shrieked Rhoda. 'He s-s-said, "The whole thing's off! It should never have begun".' Gripping Tina's hand Rhoda burst into fresh sobs. 'Jade must have been absolutely *heartbroken* hearing him say such a thing. I myself was shocked overhearing him.'

'Poor Jade,' mumured Tina, and dutifully wiped Rhoda's tears away. 'I can't help feeling Scott was overwrought and acted on impulse. Perhaps if I tried to find him and talk to him, things might yet be straightened out.' As the bride's sister she felt a certain duty in the matter.

'Oh, you won't find him at the airport,' said Rhoda, glancing at her watch. 'Scott left the country two hours ago in a private aircraft belonging to one of his business associates. He's *gone,* don't you understand? Gone and left my child in the lurch. Jilted! *Such* an insult! *What* disgrace!'

'What a brute!' said Tina furiously. A flashback of Scott entering the Zambezi with the blonde girl on his arm added fuel to her anger, although she couldn't see what it had to do with the present situation, which seemed to her at the moment rather like a mad dream. 'I can't believe this is

91

actually happening,' she said.

'Well, believe me it's true. I really don't know how I'm going to bear it.'

'Can we ring Jade?'

'The worst of it is she didn't leave a number where one could reach her out there in California. She spoke only to Scott, and he banged the phone down in the end, so I didn't get a chance to find out. Oh, he was so *rude!*'

'Betrayer!' muttered Tina, infected by Rhoda's hysteria. 'I hate myself for believing that man was really a very special person.'

'Oh, but he was!' wailed Rhoda. 'And now we've lost him!'

'We?' Tina frowned.

'The whole family.'

Tina straightened up proudly. 'Consider this a lucky escape for us. Do we really need a character like that?' she demanded dramatically.

But disconsolate Rhoda rose, sniffing, and made her way unsteadily from the room, wailing: 'I'll never live this down. Never!'

Turmoil in the house increased after Rhoda had broadcast the news that Jade's wedding was off. Mrs McCabe, who had baked and iced the wedding-cake, came promptly and took it away for sale to another bride-to-be. People rang all day at short intervals offering sympathy and practical help.

'Most of them suspect the truth that Jade's been jilted, and are secretly enjoying the sensation,' Rhoda fumed. 'My daughter has always been the victim of jealousy on account of her unusual beauty, and talent and go-ahead nature that has made her successful. I'm glad she's now in America, making a great career. At least there she is appreciated. Things may have turned out for the best after all.'

One of the many telephone calls was for Tina. From Mike Hatton, asking her out that evening.

'My stepmother needs me at home. There's a lot to be done. Undone, really.'

Rhoda 'overheard' in passing and tapped her on the shoulder, whispering 'Go! Go out with the man. Something may come of it.'

Tina accepted Mike's invitation and spent the evening with him at a cinema, then at a small restaurant where he informed her, 'I took your advice and grabbed that job offer in London. It's great to think I'll see you there. When d'you return?'

'The day after tomorrow,' she told him, making an instant decision of her own.

There seemed no point in staying on now that the wedding was cancelled. Besides, she yearned to be back home, among her own things, getting on with work and trying to forget her brief, though memorable, encounter with Scott Kyle. Despite everything, she knew he would not be easily forgotten.

And the thing she remembered quite suddenly, while Mike was kissing her goodnight, was that Scott had taken her London address. The thought clutched at her heart, causing a nervous little flutter beneath the ribs, in the same region where Mike's hand was tentatively straying. Quickly she said goodnight and slipped away, leaving him calling after her:

'Remember your promise to let me see you in London!'

In her mind she heard the voice of Scott Kyle, telling her he was glad she lived alone. Never had she felt so confused and uncertain. And afraid as well.

EIGHT

The London-bound British Airways jet rose high above Harare's runway lights and headed out into the night. Seat-belts were unfastened and Tina settled down to relax into a pleasurable state of near-normality. Already she could feel her familiar lifestyle reaching out to meet her. It was good to think that just a night's journey now separated her from all she ever wanted: her work, friends, a mini-apartment rented in a converted house owned by the mother of a friend in South Kensington.

She took one last glance through the aircraft window at the country of her childhood slipping away behind, becoming one with the vast panorama of Africa. Her brief visit was already part of the past, like the aborted wedding. Jade, her extrovert sister, would soon recover from that setback, and so would Rhoda. Which left Scott, an unkown quantity, also now in the past.

Just before leaving her stepmother's house, Rhoda had confessed to Tina that Scott had left 'a fat sum of money' to pay for expenses of the cancelled wedding.

'I felt like throwing it back in his face, but, after all, it's only fair he should make some amends. By rights he should be sued for breach of promise,' Rhoda had declared.

Tina had burned with embarrassment, but then Rhoda went on to say: 'However, he did enclose a letter with his cheque.'

'Oh — a letter?' Tina repeated with quick curiosity.

Rhoda preened herself. 'It was a very *nice* letter, I must admit. Very sympathetic towards me and all that. But, of course, that doesn't excuse what he did, running out on my daughter the way he did!'

Now, thinking back on it, Tina wondered how much of Scott's letter Rhoda was keeping to herself. And once again she felt the secret hurt she had felt at Scott's abrupt departure without a word or a brief note addressed to her personally. It was again hurtful that he had not so much as included a message for her in his note to Rhoda. Not even 'Goodbye'.

The old lady occupying the neighbouring seat in the aircraft broke into Tina's thoughts with a touch on the arm. Receiving Tina's startled glance she beamed widely and said: 'Don't you think these modern planes are just wonderful? Why, when you think of the way folks had to travel in olden times. My ancestors were Dutch colonials and had to trek over mountain ranges in oxwagons and took years over it. People must have been a lot less impatient than they are nowadays.'

Tina brought her mind vaguely to the subject and politely answered, 'Oh yes, indeed.' She hoped her neighbour would not turn out to be the over-talkative kind.

'Do you sleep well on aeroplanes?' the old lady wanted to know, instantly reminding Tina of how she had slept on Scott's shoulder on the way out. The memory was poignant now, and a little sad. How badly things had turned out!

'— Because,' her neighbour was chatting on, 'this seat on the other side of me is empty, and nobody can get on now. The next stop's Heathrow, you see. D'you think they'd mind if I stretched out when the lights are dimmed? You and I could take it in turns to share the extra space.'

'I'm fine. You just have it all for yourself,' Tina was quick to say. She began paging through the airways magazine for a while after helping the old lady to settle down comfortably. Then she herself fell asleep and had a silly dream about terrorists pouring down slopes in the Vumba Mountains to bind Scott and herself to a tree. The dream popped like a bubble when Scott said to one of the terrs, 'Help yourself to chocolates from my top right-hand pocket, Cheeza.'

Tina woke, giggling, just as the old lady beside her shook her by the arm. 'Belt-up dear. We're coming down.'

'Already?' Tina stared round in surprise.

'You were so sound asleep you missed your breakfast and it's too late now.'

In fact there was no time to wash and tidy up before landing, and she had to make do with a hasty dab of powder and lipstick and run a comb through her tumbled mass of hair. Fortunately she was not being met, so it didn't matter too much.

Her luggage, being one of the last pieces to be loaded, was amongst the first to come sweeping along the conveyor. Tina had just grabbed her passing suitcase and was about to swing it to the floor when a hand came out and took it from her.

She wheeled indignantly. 'That's mine, if you don't mind!'

'Yes, miss. I have orders to take it out for you. The car will be waiting outside.'

'Car? What car?'

'The Mercedes, miss. Pale blue.' The man recited a registration number, touched his peaked cap and melted into the crowd. Tina made efforts to recapture her case but it was hopeless trying to catch up with the man. Why were there no bobbies around when you badly needed one! Small use would it be for her to tell any one of the swarming people that she had been the victim of a confidence trick. One satisfaction was that the thief would gain nothing except some worn clothes and a new bridesmaid's dress. Obviously she had been mistaken for someone very much richer than herself, despite her name printed largely on the case.

A thought struck her: blue Mercedes? She recalled the number and wondered if she should go out and look.

The first thing that met her eyes on leaving the building was a blue Mercedes smoothly drawing up, driven by the man in the peaked cap. He barely gave her a glance, sitting there ramrod straight and unconcerned as if he had not just robbed her.

The second thing she saw as the car stopped for a moment, was the rear door nearest her swing open and an arm come out. The next minute she had been swept on to the back seat in an ambience of taped classical music and the smell of real leather. The man who had pulled her in leant across to shut the door, affording just the most discreet nuance of some musky aftershave, as his face brushed past.

It had all happened so quickly that Tina had been unable to take a proper look at her abuductor against whom she now struggled furiously: 'How dare you! Let me go at once!'

He released her suddenly and she fell against him. 'Tina,' he reasoned gently. 'Tina, I'm sorry it had to turn out like this. That was a no-stopping zone and I acted on impulse. We were held up by traffic getting here. I was afraid of missing you, which is why I sent Joe dashing off in, while I kept watch for you here.' He smiled, letting his eyes rove her face. 'Welcome home, darling.'

Tina gaped at him stunned. 'How dare you!'

He frowned down at her: 'Surely Rhoda conveyed my message? I mentioned in my note to her that I'd meet you. My friends in Harare phoned me your flight number. The grapevine, you know,' he smiled.

Tina drew a deep breath to control her trembling, and said with biting sarcasm, 'Oh, naturally I'm terribly impressed by your slick methods, Scott. *Naturally* one would expect it of you to be able to lay hands on whatever information you needed about anyone's comings and goings. As it happens, though, I'd much rather you hadn't troubled to meet me.'

'Tina!' Scott's eyes narrowed intently. Then he reached out and drew her head to his shoulder. 'Poor kid. You're tired and cross and my blundering efforts to surprise you have made things worse. I'll take you home now for a rest, and then perhaps dinner out this evening.'

Her eyes flashed contemptuously: 'Your arrogance is stunning, Scott!' She moved away from him.

He moved a bit closer. 'What have I done wrong?'

'Taken too much for granted. First you insult my sister, then you-you-you . . .'

'Tina darling, listen to me. You're tired.'

'I am *very* tired,' she said. 'Of you. Ask your chauffeur to stop this car at once, please.'

Scott brushed a hand over the back of her head. 'Perhaps after a bath and a rest you'll allow me to see you this evening? There's explaining to do.'

But now Tina was beyond reason in the aftermath of shock and in the throes of a welter of mixed emotions. 'Tell your driver to stop, please!'

When Scott did nothing, she leant forward, trembling, and gave the command herself.

Scott helped her alight and stood with her on the pavement, holding her case, asking: 'Is this all? There must be some reason, surely, for the way you're behaving. I've got to know. Please tell me.'

'There's nothing you don't already know, Scott, except that I'm *not* about to fall in line as your next playmate. In fact, I'd prefer never to see you again.' She took the case from him and walked stiffly away, anxious not to prolong the agony and perhaps betray herself.

She signalled for a cab and rode home in it, feeling not altogether pleased with the way she had handled the situation. It had, of course, taken her by surprise, and the anger against Scott, largely planted in her by Rhoda, had accounted for much. She felt further confused by the thought that Scott had given Rhoda a message — or so he said — which Rhoda had failed to deliver. Why? An uncomfortable feeling of having acted against her own better sense began to prick her conscience. And, after all, had such violent reaction been necessary?

The cabby had to inform her a second

time that they had arrived at her address. She paid him and went in.

Her normally cheerful apartment seemed as dull and listless as she herself was feeling. She dropped her case where she stood and crossed to the window with its view of drizzling rain, made all the more dreary in comparison with yesterday's bright African sunshine.

It came as a relief when the phone rang to break the silence, but the caller was only some child having a game and wanting to argue about it. Tina replaced the receiver thinking that naturally she'd never hear Scott's voice on the line. No man, least of all one with his kind of pride, would forgive the way she had put him down. She could hardly forgive herself now.

For something to do she went out to buy groceries, and on her return found mail lying on the mat. Since becoming a writer, never could she see typewritten envelopes addressed to herself, especially slim ones, without a surge of wild hope that one of her literary efforts had won a letter of acceptance. (Fat envelopes usually meant rejections.)

The envelope she chose to open first contained news that her story, sent off weeeks ago to a top woman's magazine, had been accepted for publication. Normally this would have been an occasion for unrestrained joy, but today Tina felt no more than a sedate satisfaction in the honour bestowed upon her, and a quiet sense of achievement. Her feelings were too dead at present for wild exultation. She seemed to have aged, in a way that was somehow for the better, although in a way painful. A butterfly emerging from its chrysalis.

Meanwhile, life went on; there was unpacking to be done, for instance. Leaving the remainder of the mail to read later, she took the acceptance letter and her suitcase to the bedroom. When the unpacking was done she had a long, hot bath, made a flask of coffee and got into bed, emotionally and physcially exhausted.

Her diary lay on the bedside table, the editorial letter tucked into it for recording. As Tina leant over for the diary, something fell from its pages and fluttered down the low front of her lace-trimmed nightie. Carefully she fished it out and held it in the palm of her hand. The flame lily. It glowed at her in the lamplight, a bitter-sweet reminder of Scott.

I ought to throw it away, she thought, but did nothing for a while except look at the still-fresh flower. And then, impulsively, she tucked it back into the diary and shut the book and lay holding it against her breast, eyes closed, visualising herself back in Africa. With Scott. She felt it best to let the memories run on until all was played out into nothingness. And thus, played out herself, she fell asleep.

Deep into the night the phone rang, and went on ringing with the insistent note of calamity. Tina stumbled out of bed, sleep-drugged and full of alarm. Surely nobody would call at this hour except in dire emergency!

'Hello?' she quavered into the phone.

The answer came in a high, frolicky voice: 'Hi there, Sis! How's life?'

'Jade! Are you all right?'

'Of course, silly. Why not?' followed by tinkling laughter. And then, 'I just couldn't wait to give you my wonderful, wonderful news. I'm a movie star! Just seen some of the rushes. They're great. I'm great! Life's great!'

'I'd say you sound a bit high. Champagne?' said Tina.

'Well — it's a celebration. Of my dream come true!'

'I really am awfully happy for you, Jade.'

'Oh, Tina, I just can't believe it's true. I'm in heaven!'

'Well,' said Tina, 'this will make up for the disappointment of your cancelled wedding, I suppose.'

'What?' shouted Jade cheerfully. 'Oh, *wedding!* I had to take a raincheck on that.'

'A postponement?' Tina frowned. 'But I was told — that it was all off for good.'

'Oh, you dear innocent lamb, Tina. Scott may not realise it but he will always be there for me when I'm ready for him. Meanwhile I don't grudge him his little flings. He is all man, you know.'

Tina marvelled silently at her step-sister's formidable self-confidence.

She found herself replying heatedly: 'If you want him you'd better come and get him!'

'Oh I will, darling, I will. London beckons and I'll be there on a flying visit one day. Meanwhile, wish me luck.'

'Break a leg,' said Tina obligingly.

Jade thanked her and rang off.

NINE

A spate of questions concerning her trip to Africa greeted Tina's return to work. She parried most of them with some high-sounding phrases about political affairs in her former country, which immediately damped further interest.

Fortunately, a flap broke out during the rest of the morning in regard to a deadline, and so she was spared having to make revelations about the cancelled wedding or deal with probings about her own romantic adventures.

By and large it was a hectic day, allowing her to lunch solely on a cup of coffee, and she did an hour's overtime (unpaid) at the end of it. She had stayed on from choice when the others went home, all except her friend Ginger, formally known as Miss Granger, who had hung back, pottering at the word-processer, apparently trying to extricate from its memory-system a poem she had previously entrusted to it.

Ginger finally gave up in disgust and said to Tina, 'The brute's stolen my masterpiece. I did so want you to read it, and now it's been swallowed up.'

'Probably all for the best,' said Tina, and ducked to avoid the paper-clip thrown at her.

'Have they told you the news yet?' Ginger asked.

'Is there something special?'

'Oh, yes, indeed. I thought you'd have heard by now. But perhaps you're being spared on your first day back. Have you a date for this evening?'

'No,' Tina said, stabbed by the thought of Scott. 'Have you?' She turned her back, searching through her handbag for keys.

'Not a hope,' Ginger replied bitterly. 'Lester and I have quarrelled, and this time it might be final.'

Tina took her by the arm. 'Come and cry on my shoulder at Luigi's place. I'm thirsting for a tall glass of his lemon tea.'

'Ugh! But I'll come anyway. Ravioli and double milk-shake for me. In times of misery food's my only consolation,' Ginger said dolefully.

Tina slanted an amused glance at her friend. It would take a lot to make Ginger miserable for any length of time. Her Lester was much the same. Their tiffs seemed almost self-inflicted merely to accentuate the ecstasy of reconciliation, during which flowers would be sent and coo-ing, damp-eyed telephone calls exchanged. This time, however, Ginger seemed to be unusually woebegone for some reason.

They settled on neighbouring stools at Luigi's counter and sat in silence after ordering.

'It's more than Lester, isn't it?' Tina asked eventually. 'Something really serious?'

Ginger suddenly blurted: 'There's talk of the magazine being taken over. Now that the day is done, I might as well be the one to break the ghastly news to you.'

Tina sat stunned for a moment, before speaking the first thought that came to mind: 'Just a rumour, or is it true?'

Ginger shrugged dejectedly. 'Very hush-hush at present, but it seems to be a fore-gone conclusion. Final seal yet to be set.' She hunched further forward over her plate of pasta.

'All very sudden, isn't it?' Tina said shakily.

'Well, it's being said that the power behind it is famous for his quick deals. A foreigner of some sort. I hate him!'

'What's he like?'

'Haven't set eyes on him yet. At a guess I'd say brash and brazen. Probably the type who pinches bottoms and wears T-shirts with slogans on when he sails his yacht in the Med.'

'Oh, dear.'

'Is that all you can say, for heaven's sake, Tina?'

Tina took a deep breath and shook her head. 'I'm floored.'

'Me too. What with Lester on top of it all.' Ginger turned moist eyes to Tina. 'I feel a hunch that your trip hasn't been a bed of roses. Was there a man? You look pale and languishing. Are you in love? Did it happen out there in the wilds of Africa?'

Tina decided to use Jade's cancelled wedding as a shield for her own affairs, and Ginger sat listening politely but without emotion. They dissected the wedding subject, bit by bit, over their meal, and then went out to stroll in the West End, shopgazing their way through Bond Street, meandering along Regent, returning at last to the subject uppermost in their minds — the fate of the magazine; whether the new owner might 'kill it off' to serve his own purpose, or run it under his own imprint. Whether all the present staff would have to go, or some be allowed to stay.

The magazine, a bi-monthly, had survived rough times and was now making fast headway under a small and friendly staff dedicated to maintaining a bright young concept. The figures had begun to show steadily increasing sales which seemed firmly set on the upward course. And now this! Tina felt a smouldering fury against the organisation responsible for making a grab at something she cared so much about.

The next day she plucked up courage and tackled Rosamund direct in the privacy of her executive office. Ms Rosamund Hickey owned the magazine and had fought along gamely to keep it going. Lately she had taken a partner to run the business side of things, a handsome Canadian and provider of funds, who was also her newly-acknowledged fiancé.

'Rosie,' said Tina. 'It's shocking that you might be selling out to some stranger after the way we've all pulled together, and at a time when results are coming in.'

Rosie swivelled back in her chair: 'I know just how you feel. But there's a lot to be considered. This offer is far to good to refuse, and in the interests of my staff — all you darling people — as well as for the benefit of the magazine, it would be wrong of me to reject it. As it is, everyone will be staying on in their present jobs, except me. Nothing will change, in fact everything will improve with more finance to back us. Back you, I mean. I'll be out.'

'No!' cried Tina idignantly. 'We won't stand your being thrown out by some interloper —'

Rosie held up her hand. 'You've got it a bit wrong. Actually I'm leaving from choice. I'll be getting married and leaving for Canada after the deal is through. I've been offered a sub-editorial position on one of the leading women's magazines out there. It will be a wonderful challenge for me and I'm looking forward to it. Sit down and join me in a cup of coffee.'

'Congratulations, but I won't stay.' Tina felt cold and empty. 'The magazine won't be the same without you, Rosie.'

'Oh, I —' Rosie bit back the rest and snatching up a handkerchief left the room abruptly.

Tina felt like crying too. Nothing would ever be the same again, she felt. The rug had been pulled from underfoot, the old order disturbed. It remained to be seen whether it would all turn out for the better.

Later Ginger said to her, 'You're over-reacting, the way we all did at first. Let's give it a chance and see what happens, you know.'

Tina returned home that evening to find a letter from Mike Hatton awaiting her. In it he said he had accepted the job offered him in London and would be arriving from Zimbabwe the following week. He 'hoped it would be O.K.' to call on her, and asked for a reply letting him know if she agreed.

Tina laid aside the letter with a twinge of irritation. Scott would never have minded whether she agreed or not. He would just arrive. And probably whisk her off to some romantic place for dinner. And she could confide in him how bad she was feeling about the magazine, and be consoled by his own indignation that such an unfair thing should happen.

Coming down to earth from this daydream was like a bad parachute-landing. It left her shaken by her own foolishness in bringing on thoughts of Scott to torment herself. He belonged to the past, as Tina so often assured herself sternly and resolutely. Yet somehow he would not stay there, as if time and distance meant nothing when it came to a matter of yearning thoughts. There was no point in denying to herself that she did yearn for him.

The next morning, in the thick of her work, the phone rang and when she answered it her heart suddenly thumped. 'Scott!' she said hoarsely.

'You have a cold?' he asked.

'No, of course not!'

'Well, I just thought I'd find out how you are.'

'I'm just fine, thank you.'

'Good. Then perhaps we could get together for a chat.'

'A chat about what?' she asked.

'The magazine, for one thing.'

'I'm not sure I understand what you mean, Scott.'

'Would you let me explain over dinner tonight. Just the two of us?'

'Why not right now over the telephone?' she asked.

'Because the subject calls for candlelight and roses.'

'I don't think Jade would approve.'

'Jade's not involved in my business affairs.'

A cold suspicion took hold of Tina. For the moment it left her speechless, and Scott, taking advantage of her struggle for words, cajoled winningly: 'Say yes. Please? Good. I'll be round for you at your place about eight.'

The persuasive timbre of that deep, husky

voice cut through her resistance like a hot knife through butter. She hated herself for not refusing, and tried to pass off her weakness as being due to curiosity about what he might have to tell her regarding the magazine. What diabolic cunning on his part, dangling a carrot like that! Beneath the surface of her immediate reaction, however, lay a kinder, softer layer of pleasure at the thought of seeing him again. Her heart all at once took flight.

Scott arrived at her apartment promptly on time. She had drilled herself to display just the right degree of cool acknowledgement, but what threw her off keel was to see him there on the doorstep holding a sheaf of flame lilies. Blushing with surprise and pleasure she accepted the flowers with murmured thanks and stood aside for him to enter, originally having planned *not* to let him in.

'You shouldn't have,' she said, looking at the lilies. 'But they're lovely.'

'I had them specially flown out for you, rather expecting you might throw them at me if it so happened I was still out of favour.'

'I'll put them in water,' she turned away, ignoring the last of his remark.

When she returned, he quite simply held out his arms and said, 'It's wonderful seeing you again, Tina.' And she somehow quite simply, accidentally almost, walked straight into his embrace. Scott's arms tightened round her suddenly and his mouth covered hers in fierce, hungry eagerness, drawing from her a response at first unwilling and then all at once desirous and tender.

The quality of Scott's kiss grew gentler as his hand stroked her shoulder, moved caressingly down to the curve of her breast, but then she stiffened in his arms and pushed him away. 'No!' she gasped, her eyes feverish-bright.

'What is it, Tina? Why are you so furious with me?' Scott made no further attempt to touch her but stood where she had left him. 'Why?' he asked again.

'Because you brutally jilted my sister. And insulted the whole family. Made fools of them. Publicly.'

'Oh?' His eyes narrowed, developing a steely glint. 'Well, if that's what you think then it's time for an explanation.'

'. . . And,' she continued, as if he hadn't spoken, 'and you rudely left the house without so much as bidding me a decent word of goodbye.'

'Goodbye is not a decent word at all. I loathe the very sound of it.' Scott's mouth twisted as he spoke.

'And now you're here, behaving as if nothing had happened, ringing me up at work, dropping mysterious hints about the magazine. Presumably *my* magazine, the source of my — my livelihood!' Tina realised she was running on at random but seemed unable to check her indignation. 'The magazine means a great deal to me!'

'I know,' said Scott gravely. 'Which is why I — I've just clinched the deal. I bought it for you, Tina, rather than let someone else have it merely to kill it off.'

She stared at him, her lips parted in shocked disbelief, and couldn't find a single word to say. *He* was the new owner?

Scott lifted her wrap from one of the chairs and tenderly folded it around her. 'Come on, let's go celebrate.'

Tina allowed him to lead her away, his arm gently round her waist.

She stopped suddenly and looked up at him.

'Scott?'

'Yes, Tina?'

'How did you know I cared so much about the magazine?'

'I had long talks with Rhoda. All about you, and your work, and the kind of person you are. Not that Rhoda understands much about you, but I do.'

'Oh? How can you possibly, on such short acquaintance?'

'Twin souls know one another from the start, Tina. We are two of a kind. I don't think it's necessary to tell you that.'

She lowered her eyes, knowing just what he meant.

TEN

Tina sat unmindful of Piccadilly's bright
lights glittering through a shimmer of rain.
the windscreen wiper's metronome rhythm
seemed to make her conscious only of
Scott's vibrant presence beside her, as if
just being there, behind the driving wheel
of his luxury car, gave him hypnotic rights
over her mind. She sank further into the
spell, a ladybird caught in a spider's web. A
willing victim, though.

When the car stopped and Scott crossed
over to open the door for her and draw her
out to the pavement, the touch of his hand
on her bare arm startled her to life. At once
he gathered her up against him and they
quickstepped through the rain to be wel-
comed into an interior of warm lighting,
soft music and magical fragrances.

Tina regained her wits and noticed how
carefully the effects had been arranged at
their table. Champagne stood chilling in a

silver bucket and between two tall candle-sticks was placed a crystal bowl of flowers whose colours leapt to life when a waiter lit the candles. Red roses. Emblems of love.

Glancing up she met Scott's smiling eyes. 'Gerrit would have been able to provide the right music,' he said, waiting for her to be seated. 'But at least I contributed the flowers. They seemed just right for you and the occasion.'

She dipped her fingertips lightly amidst the crisp petals, releasing a wave of perfume, and remembered what Jade had said over the phone: 'Scott may not realise it, but he will always be there for me when I'm ready for him.'

Conscious of Scott's watchful eyes Tina glanced up and said, casually: 'I had a call from Jade.'

He nodded: 'So did I. But this is your evening, not Jade's. Shall we just forget her for the time being?'

Tina continued to gaze thoughtfully into his eyes for some moments before saying: 'Jade isn't easily forgettable. You should know that.'

He raised a sardonic eyebrow and shrugged: 'What I do know right now is that you're looking stunning this evening. That black dress suits you.'

The waiter poured their wine and left. Scott raised his glass to her: 'To our future.' But Tina found she could not enter into the spirit while the haunting thought presented itself that this was what he should have been doing back there in Zimbabwe — toasting Jade, his bride, after their wedding. As he might yet be doing some day, not too far off. When Jade got him back!

'Come on, snap out of it, Tina. Aren't you at all pleased about the magazine?'

'I'm absolutely overwhelmed,' she said quickly. 'It's still hard to believe that you should have taken the trouble to do such a wonderful thing. At great expense, I'm sure. So magnificent of you.'

He was looking at her suspiciously. 'Do I detect a shade of sarcasm?'

'Why no, Scott, no. It's just that I feel so beholden to you. Deeply indebted. Because you say you bought the magazine for me.'

'And because I know you're going to make a success of it.'

She released a long breath. 'I'll try.'

'But?' he cocked an eyebrow. 'You're afraid I might demand payment for the favour?'

'It's usually what does happen when men give women expensive gifts.'

She saw a glint of anger in his eyes as

Scott answered, 'If that's the way you feel, then stop thinking of it as a gift. All I shall ask you to be is a good employee, working for the good of my investment. Right? Fine. Then let's drink the toast.'

Her fingers remained on the stem of her neglected wineglass until Scott placed his hand over hers and lifted the wine to her lips. 'I swear to make you trust me, Tina, to take that look of uncertainty from your eyes. I won't rest until it's done. And now let's dance?'

She hadn't realised how much she had wanted to be in his arms until he gathered her close. The warning voice inside her that said, 'Beware!' went ignored as her body melted against his to the beat of the music and she moved dreamily with him into a withdrawn world of their own.

It came as a wrench when Scott, dropping a quick kiss on her forehead, led her back to their waiting meal. She felt mesmerised, and a little worried at her weakening resistance to the magnetic influence over her of a man who, until lately almost a stranger, had now become so important in her life.

She toyed with her excellent lobster thermidor and surreptitiously watched Scott eating neatly and competently, enjoying every mouthful with manly appetite. How different he looked tonight from the man in safari clothes in the wilds of his former country where she had felt more akin to him than now, in this elegant restaurant that matched his lifestyle as a successful entrepreneur, a man who had apparently made a fortune and had invested some of it in her career. She suspected he had done the same for Jade, boosting her as a model, placing her amidst influential people in films. Asking her to marry him. And then — ?

And then striding away to his own kind of world, free and unfettered, to find new companions, fresh fields to conquer, other girls and their careers to promote. Was that what he was all about? She wished she knew for certain.

Scott suddenly looked up and in that compelling way of his, captured her eyes. 'What are we going to do, Tina?'

'About what, Scott?'

'About us. Are we falling in love?'

'I'm not experienced enough to judge.' She laughed a light, teasing little ripple of laughter intended to convey indifference.

Scott held her eyes seriously: 'Should nothing be done about it?'

Tina shook her head and lowered her lashes. 'Nothing. Most probably it will pass — like it did with you and Jade.'

'You've decided to torture me.' The tone of Scott's voice made her glance up and catch her breath at the grim look of displeasure on his face. As if he might get up and walk off, leaving her alone. Instead he took her hand and led her back to the crowded dance-floor, into a dim-lit world of romantic unreality where the supposition that they were in love seemed almost true.

They danced through half the night, going on to a different place, and yet another, until Tina asked to be taken home. Scott suggested going to his place first, but she told him 'No'.

He was in a mood now, brooding silently over secret thoughts. Then, in answer to her 'No' he said, 'I've no ulterior motives. It's just that I would have liked you to have visited my kia, even for the shortest time.'

Hearing him call his apartment a kia, the African name for a hut or living-place, forced a quick laugh from Tina and she felt the warm and friendly bond between them, dating back to a past shared in childhood.

'All right,' she said, relaxing. 'Let me inspect your kia.'

He thanked her with a hard squeeze of her hand, sending the familiar tingle of excitement darting through her.

His apartment had its own private elevator that gave access to a small lobby leading to a spacious living-room. Tina had half-expected to see animal skins or other relics of Africa on display but there were none. The striking oil-painting that caught her eye at once was an original Gauguin, painted in Tahiti, its golden tints picked out in a large hand-woven dhurrie of Indian origin covering an area of polished floor on which stood superbly comfortable-looking lounging furniture.

From the dim recesses of the room there came a sudden howl and a wild rush of animal life. One animal, in a state of high excitement. Simba, by the looks of it.

'Look out, you! There's a lady present,' said Scott, receiving the onslaught with a tolerant grin. 'Sit down, Tina, before he bowls you over.'

Tina quickly obeyed, asking, 'What's he doing here in this apartment?'

'Enjoying himself immensely. I take him for regular visits to the country, when time permits, of course. He loves it on the estate.'

'What estate?'

'Mine,' Scott said, transferring the dog's attention to her as he himself moved off towards a coffee-percolator. 'I have this place in Hertfordshire, you see.'

'Ah,' said Tina, nodding. Naturally, he would!

'I run it as a farm,' Scott said, 'with the help of a few ex-Rhodesians whose special skills stand in good stead.'

Tina's attention was claimed by Simba who leapt on to the divan, almost into her lap. She addressed Scott while trying to cope with the dog: 'I'm surprised Rhoda allowed you to have Simba sent over here.'

'She might have paid me to do it, I believe, except this is not *that* Simba. I acquired him at Cruft's a couple of years ago. He once belonged to someone who started a bloodline here in England.' Scott placed two small cups of Turkish coffee and two glasses of liqueur on the table at hand, and heaving Simba out of the way, sat down beside her, laying his arm across the back of the settee, lightly touching her bare shoulders. His closeness had the same mesmeric effect on her as she had felt earlier.

'What was the meaning of that knowing look you gave me when I mentioned the farm?' Scott asked.

Tina collected her thoughts and replied, 'You called it an estate and I thought it natural for a tycoon like you to have such a place. Don't they all?'

He was smiling down at her as if at a

charming child. 'I wouldn't really know about them all. Myself, I'm no tycoon. Just a hard-working guy trying to make an honest buck. And this is a very boring subject. Let's change it.'

'You lead,' she said, nonchalantly, and by way of reply Scott gathered her into his arms, placing his lips on hers.

Tina closed her eyes and felt she could almost hear soft sweet music in the air and smell the night fragrances of a Rhodesian garden, as on that first night Scott had kissed her. This time she was swept ever further away from any attempt at restraint and gave herself fully to the rapture of the moment, and to Scott's dangerously ardent kiss.

Her arms slowly and sensuously crept round his neck, her fingers playing through his thick, dark hair. His sharp intake of breath might have registered on her senses as a warning, had her senses at that moment not been too pleasurably engrossed to notice.

Suddenly his arms were crushing her against himself, his mouth bruising hers. She felt his hand slip under the delicate bootlace straps of her dress, drawing it off her shoulders. Then his lips were there, pressing kisses along the curve of her throat, down to her gleaming white shoulders, and lower as the black dress slipped halfway to her waist.

For a few exquisite moments Tina lay back amongst the cushions letting Scott have his way, his gentle hands ardently caressing, drawing helpless little moans from her, his lips burning her flesh. Then, with a supreme effort, she caught his fingers and tried to push him away. He did not resist her, but whispered against her lips, 'Don't leave me now. Please stay.'

The urgency in his voice, the words of a proposition unexpected from him — foolishly unexpected — brought her sadly down to earth. Slipping out of his arms she stood up breathlessly.

'I'm sorry, Scott. I'm just not the fast-lane type.' She gazed at him, limpid-eyed, longing to rush back into his embrace. 'I — simply — *can't!*' she ended fiercely, and snatched up her things on the way out.

Scott had risen to his feet, but made no effort to stop her. She looked back from the door of the elevator and saw him standing there, the dog at his side, watching her go. It piqued her that not even the dog had accompanied her to the door. As if they both condemned her as a prude.

■ ■ ■ ■

Tina decided over the next few days that she would have to resign her position on the magazine. To stay on as matters stood between herself and Scott would amount to accepting a favour from him while refusing the kind of repayment he had obviously been expecting. Sometimes, at the back of her mind, was a niggling suspicion that she might be misjudging him, and yet since he had made no attempt to contact her since her flight from his apartment, it appeared she was no longer important to him — except as an employee whose resignation was overdue! It was necessary, however, for the takeover to be made official first. Meanwhile, to keep thoughts of Scott at bay, she threw herself feverishly into a pile of work.

At the end of another week of silence from Scott, her doorbell rang one evening, making her heart leap to the sound. Carefully controlling an impulse to rush in answer, she took her time composing herself before slowly opening the door. The image of the man she expected to see slowly dissolved into bitter disappointment.

There, on the mat, stood Mike Hatton, beaming at her and somehow looking quite out of place. 'I lost my way, of course, but here I am at last.'

Dazedly Tina stepped back for him to enter, murmuring some formal phrase of welcome as he did so, seeming to bring in with him a gust of African air straight off the Zimbabwean high veld.

'Boy! This drizzling rain! Does it never stop?' he complained cheerfully, holding Tina's hand, feasting his eyes on her. 'I arrived this morning. Couldn't wait to see you. Should have phoned. Hope you don't mind?'

'Don't be silly,' Tina tried to sound brisk and pleased. 'Sit down I'll get coffee.'

'Wait just a minute.' He fished in his pocket. 'Here, I brought you this little something.'

Tina accepted the package he thrust at her awkwardly, asking her to open it at once.

Undoing the brown-paper wrapping revealed a brown cardboard box, and in the box a jagged piece of rock.

Mike burst out laughing at her look of surprise. 'I imagined you'd accept it as a suitable gift from a geologist,' he said. 'It's a chunk of your one-time native land, Tina. To use as a paper-weight, or whatever, and remind you of me, I hope.'

She smiled at him. 'How original. I love

it,' and was about to set it on the coffee-table when Mike stopped her. 'No, no. Turn it over first. This piece is from an emerald-mine I recently discovered on my little parcel of land.'

Placing his hand over hers he gave her wrist a gentle twist that brought round the reverse side of the rock, showing an embedded bright-green stone.

'An emerald? But you can't give me this!' Tina gasped. 'It must be worth a small fortune!'

'Hardly good enough for you,' Mike said, standing there gazing at her with his heart in his eyes and at the same time so shy and awkward that Tina raised her arms and drew down his cheek to her own for a moment. 'Thank you for your kindness, Mike.'

He seemed stunned for a moment and then quickly his arms closed round her, making her instantly regret her impulsive gesture which had given a wrong impression, now too late to correct. Mike had her so ardently clasped to himself that she could feel the alarming beat of his heart and the rapid quickening of his breath.

She pushed him aside with a false little laugh. 'Heavens! The coffee must be boiling over!' She rushed off to kitchen, with Mike following behind in a rather dazed state.

He tried to help her with the coffee and in their flustered condition they made a hash of things.

'Look,' Mike said, 'let's forget it, and you come over with me to my hotel for a drink instead. We could have a chat before dinner. After all, this is quite a red-letter day for me, finding myself in London at last and seeing you again into the bargain.'

While Tina hesitated, Mike took the gap: 'Come on, I kept the taxi waiting.'

'I need time to change.'

'I'll wait.' He dumped himself in a chair and waited.

That evening with Mike turned out to be fun. After a drink and a meal they took in a show for which he had come armed with tickets, and then they moved on to a little place by the river, run by a friend of his from home. They danced to accordion music and met some Zimbabwean friends, which made it a very late night in the end.

Mike did no more than hold her hand when they said goodnight. 'What are you doing tomorrow, seeing it's Saturday? Today, really.'

'I intend to sleep until afternoon,' she answered, suppressing a yawn.

'Evening then? I have more theatre tickets.'

There was no commitment in seeing Mike

almost every evening, she argued with herself several days later. His goodnight kisses now were cool, almost brotherly, and gradually she was lured into deeper waters without realising it, until one evening, after he had stopped using taxis for transport and had bought himself a modest car in which they had driven to the country to sit watching the full moon, he took her in his arms and began to kiss her in a not at all brotherly fashion.

'What's wrong?' he asked when she gently pushed him away. 'Am I repulsive to you! Don't you see how much you mean to me?'

It burst on her then that all these evenings, by innocuous degrees he had been leading her down the road to romance; and she, blinded by thoughts of Scott, had not noticed the snare ahead.

Now, as she sat unable to answer his questions, Mike went on to say, 'I haven't wanted to rush you, but the truth is that my fortunes have improved to the extent that I can now afford a wife. And the girl I want is you, Tina. This became obvious to me from the moment I met you.'

He twisted awkwardly towards her and went down on one knee in the cramped space of the car: 'Will you marry me, Tina?'

Thinking it over in bed late that night she felt slightly hysterical at the unexpected comedy of the situation. Then she was annoyed at allowing herself to be misled about his true feelings and in the end having to hurt him. Finally she felt a depressing sense of guilt and even ingratitude towards someone so kind and likeable as Mike.

She had asked Mike, very gently, not to get in touch with her again, but he promised no more than to give her time to think over her decision. And so, as the days passed, every ring of the telephone in her apartment became a dread to her.

The time it finally rang — very late at night — she snatched up the receiver and snapped: 'Mike, this is unfair. You promised not to —'

'Sorry to disappoint you, honey, it's me,' piped her step-sister, loud and clear. 'Here I am in London, having a whale of a party at the hotel. Do come over and join us, please love? I'll send someone round to fetch you.'

Tina had no time to protest before the line went dead. However, not wanting to be caught in night clothes by whoever Jade was sending over, she quickly changed into a dress just before the doorbell rang. Answering it brought a shock.

'Hello,' Scott greeted her cheerfully. 'Nice to see you, again.'

ELEVEN

'You're looking lovely,' Scott said softly and huskily.

Tina could think of no suitable reply while she stood searching his face, her thoughts in a state of chaos. Was Jade back in London to make up their quarrel? Was she here to marry him? The party was perhaps a celebration of their being together again. She wished she had given some excuse for not going.

Scott placed his hand under her elbow; 'Well, shall we be off? You know how Jade hates being kept waiting,' he said, tongue in cheek.

Tina heard herself saying, 'After all, I don't feel like attending a party.'

'You mean not with me,' Scott sighed. 'Yes, I see. Well, congratulations. I hear you're practically engaged to old Mike Hatton. Cheer up then, he's already at the party.' While speaking, Scott had been gradually leading her out, and then slammed the door behind them. Tina, in a state of semi-somnambulation, made no protest.

They had driven just a short distance when Scott said crisply:

'You haven't denied it, I notice.'

'What?'

'Your engagement to Hatton. It's true, then?'

'I don't see that it's any concern of yours.'

'It is, you know. I can't imagine how he managed to swipe you from under my nose. Perhaps if I hadn't been called away on business to America after we last met, it wouldn't have happened.'

Tina made no reply while it sank into her mind that he'd been away.

'Are you mad about geology?' Scott asked sarcastically. 'What happened to your writing career, may I ask?'

'It happens to be flourishing,' she replied absently.

'Glad to hear it. Which means, I hope, that you'll be staying on at the magazine?'

She glanced at him sidelong. A cold look. 'You mean on your pay-roll, by special favour?'

'My dear girl, how little you seem to understand business matters. Your earned income will be provided by the company, not by me personally. Not that I wouldn't dearly love to supplement that income, if you'd let me.'

'I thought I'd made my feelings in the matter quite clear the last time we met,' Tina said primly.

'Oh you did, indeed you did, very forcefully. But —'

'Nothing's changed since then. I still have nothing for sale, except my work.'

'Ouch!' he joked, making Tina wonder if he had been drinking too much. Or was he deriding her primness? Compared with Jade, she must seem a proper mouse.

Then, suddenly serious, he brought the car to a stop against the kerb and looked intently at her by streetlight.

'Did you really think I was proposing — er — what might be called an immoral liaison between us?'

'You as good as made that plain when we last met.'

'Or so you thought.'

'Perhaps I'm stupid, but it sounded to me as if you just repeated the offer.'

Noticing that the car was stationary outside the steps of a residence, Tina wrenched open the door and got out.

Sounds of music and laughter floated out from the house, indicating that a party was in full swing. When Scott joined her she turned to him and said, 'Jade said the party was at an hotel.'

Scott's hand was under her elbow again. 'We moved on since then.' He drew her forward up the steps and into a lobby banked with lifts. Only then, after he had shown her into one of them and pressed the button, did she realise they were in his own apartment building.

'Let me out!' she turned and fumed at him. 'You've played a trick on me!'

Scott gazed down at her in surprise. 'If I didn't know better, I'd say you have a very suspicous mind.'

The lift stopped, its doors slid open and Scott handed her out into the noise and laughter. 'Your sister is somewhere in this crowd.'

Tina was left, pink with embarrassment, watching Scott walk away from her and disappear from sight before she could apologise for her impulsive accusation, which must have made it even more obvious to him that in matters of jetset society she was quite wet behind the ears. Their parties *travelled* apparently. How gauche to think otherwise!

She was thinking of going straight back home when Jade came hurtling through the crowd, squeaking with pleasure and excitement in that amusing way of hers.

After they had pecked each other gingerly in deference to Jade's carefully perfect make-up, they stood back at arm's length to examine one another.

'You're more beautiful than ever,' Tina said, admiring her step-sister's huge dark eyes, set slightly aslant, her cascading dark hair and lean, elegant body sheathed in haute couture.

'And you haven't changed a bit!' squeaked Jade ambiguously, and went on to ask, j'How was Zim— Zim— whatever they call Rhodesia these days?'

'Changed quite a bit, but still nice,' Tina told her.

'You'll never guess,' said Jade, 'how very much I have to tell you. So thrilling!'

'I'm sure,' replied Tina absently, gazing round the sea of faces. None belonged to Scott.

'Is it on again with you and your fiancé?' she asked Jade.

'But of course, darling. I told you I'd get him back. It was just a silly old storm in an egg-cup.'

'Teacup.'

'Whatever. I owe Scott a great deal. We'll marry when time permits. And now come meet my lovely American friends.' Grabbing Tina's hand Jade dragged her into the thick of things, but almost at once became diverted from her original intention and Tina found herself adrift on her own in strange company where they spoke a jargon quite above her head. She ought, she thought, to listen and learn and memorise dialogue for future literary use, except that it was like being in a parrot-house with every bird giving voice at once.

At last someone speaking ordinary English came up to her. Rather disappointingly, it turned out to be Mike Hatton, glass in hand and far too merry of mood.

'Great to see they're friends again, isn't it?' he gushed.

'Yes,' said Tina quietly, knowing he meant Jade and Scott.

Mike waved his glass and swayed very slightly: 'The next wedding is planned to take place right here in London, Scott tells me.'

'Good.' Tina felt a shaft of misery strike through her heart. The sight of Mike's inebriated grin was infuriating in the circumstances of her own abysmal depression.

'Hasn't anyone brought you a drink?' he asked.

She shook her head. 'No. I'm not staying.'

'Then I'll take you home.'

'I don't need taking.' Tina shook off his guiding hand, but Mike insisted, and in his present condition might have made a scene, so she allowed him to escort her down to the street.

They rode to her place by cab. On the doorstep he pleaded for a cup of strong coffee and she reluctantly let him in, seeing that he obviously needed help in sobering up, havingly openly admitted that he was not used to champagne.

When Tina returned with the coffee, Mike was stretched out on the settee, fast asleep and snoring gently. She drank the coffee herself, covered him with a rug and went to bed.

Halfway through the night the doorbell rang, and kept on ringing until she slipped into a wrap and went to answer it. Opening it on the chain at first, she enquired who was there.

'Scott,' came the answer.

Tina's heart began to gallop, but she called back quite composedly, 'You can't come in.'

'Why not?'

'It's far too late.'

'I'm coming in if I have to break this door down.' And he gave it a boisterous thump.

Tina capitulated, angrily opening the door and beginning to say, 'What makes you think —' But Scott came in at once, pushing her gently aside with his eyes fixed on the settee.

'Who's that?' He glared at the rug-covered figure.

For the moment Tina had quite forgotten about Mike. Following the direction of Scott's glare, she was at first surprised to see her sleeping guest.

Scott strode over and pulled back the covering. 'Ha! I see it's your fiancé. Spending the night, eh?' He dropped the rug over Mike's face but the sleeper made no stir.

Scott and Tina faced one another, she colouring with indignation and embarrassment mixed. 'You've no right to come barging in here doing as you please, Scott!'

'Right. I'm sorry I interrupted — er — something. Forgive me.'

'Why did you come?' she asked shakily.

Scott took a step closer to her. 'To talk.'

Tina felt her knees begin to tremble at the look in his eyes which seemed halfway between a caress and anger.

'What can be so important to talk about at this hour?' She drew the wrap closer about herself, feeling a little afraid of him now.

'Any hour's the right time for what there is to say,' Scott said.

'About what?' Tina stepped back from him uncertainly.

'About you and me.'

'Oh, you mean to talk business? Can't wait until morning?'

She half-suspected he might be slightly drunk. Not as far out perhaps as poor Mike, but somewhat off keel, perhaps, and so it would be wise to humour him out of the apartment. 'Maybe you should go home and sleep it off, Scott.'

'*Sleep?* Are you out of your mind?'

Scott took another step forward. 'I hoped to persuade you to listen to me. Evidently it's too late,' he gestured towards the settee. 'I had no idea things had gone so far between you and — him. If only you could understand how hard it is for me to accept.' Scott ran a hand through his tousled hair and swore softly. 'Tina, for heaven's sake, do you really love the fellow?'

Tina felt momentarily triumphant. Having the upper hand was pleasant.

'I can understand how hard it must be not having your own way as usual, Scott. It's become a habit for you to expect that. Losing is not in your book of words, is it?'

'Losing *you* certainly isn't,' he said bitterly, and aimed a frustrated kick at the settee. Mike slept on.

'Don't be adolescent,' Tina admonished calmly. 'If you've had too much champagne I can offer you some hot black coffee.'

'A pretty rotten substitute,' he grated, turning away. Tina hoped he was about to leave, but he whirled back to her.

'Are you quite sure?'

'About what?'

'That you won't have me instead?'

Her hesitation, following shock, encouraged him to press on, placing his hands on her shoulders, drawing her nearer until their lips were barely an inch apart.

'Tina darling,' he whispered hoarsely, searching her face in a way that made her glow all over. 'I'm making allowances for the fact that you're probably still too young to realise that a lifetime's happiness should not be thrown away because of some slight disagreement.'

'*Slight* dis—' she began, but he interrupted by touching her lips briefly with his own.

When she was quiet he continued: 'Back there in Rh— Zimbabwe, it was the real thing between us. Right from the start. You felt it too, didn't you?'

'I certainly felt that you were not being

exactly loyal to your bride-to-be,' she retorted with spirit. 'You were having a try at playing around. With me. Taking advantage of Jade's absence. Is that what you call the real thing? Juggling with a woman's feelings?'

'Exactly whose feelings do you mean?' he demanded.

'My sister's. And mine. You yourself don't seem to have any sensitivities!' Tina lashed out. It was a relief saying what she felt.

Scott said, 'So at last we're getting somewhere.'

'I don't think so!' she denied. 'You're still manoeuvring to have your cake and eat it.'

A sudden wild expression came into Scott's eyes, an expression of hope, almost. 'Now I see what the trouble has been. You've jumped to the conclusion that, that —' He broke off, running a hand through his hair. 'Oh, tell me about it, baby. Tell me what you've been thinking all this time.'

'Very well,' she snapped, her eyes flashing, but all the time her heart aching with love for the man. 'It's plain enough that after jilting Jade you hoped to have an affair with me by placing me under an obligation to you as far as my job is concerned. You heard the mag might have to shut down and so put two and two together. You perhaps did

146

the same with Jade. Promoted her career, pushed her up to success with promises of marriage if she played your game, and then you tired of it, didn't you? Decided to look around, and saw me. Then you dropped Jade so callously.'

'No,' Scott said quietly. 'Jade dropped me. I saw it coming, mind you. Once she got lucky in America there was no holding her. It was the career she wanted, not marriage to me. I soon began to feel we were not meant for each other after all. She told me over the phone in Zimbabwe that she looked upon our engagement as a publicity stunt. We broke it off by mutual consent and I left in a hurry rather than wait to hear Rhoda's lamentations. It was not Jade I regretted losing but you. There'll never be anyone else for me.'

He passed, lowering his mouth closer to hers. 'I want you more than you'll ever know, Tina. I need you very badly.' He tenderly caressed her face, her hair, her shoulders from which he drew down the nightdress she wore. 'The thought of you has been haunting me night and day,' he murmured, pressing her body against his own.

Tina's arms slid round his neck as she closed her eyes to his long, passionate kiss which brought out her latent fire in abandoned moments of sheer ecstasy.

Scott's urgent whisper burned against her throat. 'I adore you, Tina. Please marry me. Now. Today. I took the liberty of arranging a special licence. We could fly to Paris for our honeymoon.'

Tina gave a long deep sigh.

'Say yes — please say yes, darling,' Scott spoke against her lips.

On the settee Mike suddenly sat up and stared at them. 'Good grief! What day is it?'

'A wedding-day,' Scott told him, tightening his arms around Tina.

Tina dreamily said 'Yes' in answer to Scott's question.

Mike lay back painfully and closed his eyes. 'I could use some hot black coffee.' Instantly he was asleep again.

When Tina was dressed, Scott took her away. They left a note saying, 'Gone to get married. Back in a month.'

We hope you have enjoyed this Large Print book. Other Thorndike, Wheeler, and Chivers Press Large Print books are available at your library or directly from the publishers.

For information about current and upcoming titles, please call or write, without obligation, to:

Publisher
Thorndike Press
295 Kennedy Memorial Drive
Waterville, ME 04901
Tel. (800) 223-1244

or visit our Web site at:

www.gale.com/thorndike
www.gale.com/wheeler

OR

Chivers Large Print
published by BBC Audiobooks Ltd
St James House, The Square
Lower Bristol Road
Bath BA2 3SB
England
Tel. +44(0) 800 136919
email: bbcaudiobooks@bbc.co.uk
www.bbcaudiobooks.co.uk

All our Large Print titles are designed for easy reading, and all our books are made to last.